Praise for *One*

"Brilliant and beautiful. O... fectly executed gem of a book. Deeply satisfying and completely mesmerizing, it's full of depth, heart, and thought."
—Sarah Beth Durst, author of *The Spellshop*

"Once you start reading, it is impossible to look away from Mary Thompson's provocative story of simulations, power imbalance, and whether kindness can overcome cruelty in the end."
—Carolyn Ives Gilman, author of *Dark Orbit*

"*One Level Down* is a captivating read that you'll be tempted to tear through in one long sitting. It's also a thought-provoking book that will stay with you well beyond its final page."
—David Ebenbach, author of *How to Mars*

"Thompson shows us what kind of perfect jail software and servers can make, and how even there an inmate can dream of, and attempt, escape."
—Jack Campbell, author of *The Lost Fleet*

"A fascinating mix of mystery, thriller, and alternate futures. I had trouble putting it down."
—Stina Leicht, author of *Persephone Station*

"Riveting. . . . While Mary G. Thompson brings new insight to the nested realities of the simulation hypothesis, this is above all a story of courage as Ella risks everything to become herself."
—James Patrick Kelly, author of *Burn*

"A simulation scenario that digs deeper than the *Matrix* movies ever did; a stark portrayal of the unmitigated evil that is the parental impulse; a rapture-of-the-nerds drive-by."
—Peter Watts, Hugo Award–winning author of *The Freeze-Frame Revolution*

"*One Level Down* is a riveting existential and emotional rollercoaster, descending into the monstrous depths of patriarchy and rising into the dauntingly infinite possibilities of liberation. A brilliantly told mind-bender you won't soon forget."
—Elly Bangs, author of *Unity*

"Like the best episodes of *Black Mirror*, *One Level Down* will have you pondering the questions it raises long after you've turned the last page."
—Diana Peterfreund, author of the *Clue Mysteries* and *For Darkness Shows the Stars*

ONE LEVEL DOWN

MARY G. THOMPSON

Other Books by Mary G. Thompson

Young Adult
    The Word (2024)
    Flicker and Mist (2017)
    Amy Chelsea Stacie Dee (2016)

Middle-Grade
    Evil Fairies Love Hair (2014)
    Wulftoom (2012)
    Escape from the Pipe Men! (2013)

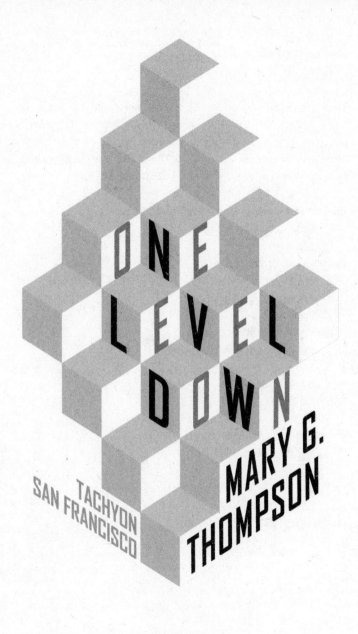

ONE LEVEL DOWN

MARY G. THOMPSON

TACHYON
SAN FRANCISCO

One Level Down

Interior and cover design by Elizabeth Story
Author photo by Can Ertoğan

Tachyon Publications LLC
1459 18th Street #139
San Francisco, CA 94107
415.285.5615
www.tachyonpublications.com
tachyon@tachyonpublications.com

Series editor: Jacob Weisman
Editor: Jaymee Goh

Print ISBN: 978-1-61696-430-6
Digital ISBN: 978-1-61696-431-3

Printed in the United States by Versa Press, Inc.

First Edition: 2025
9 8 7 6 5 4 3 2 1

1

OUR TEACHER, Camilla Wolkowitz, has driven us in the truck to the edge of the forest. By the time we reach the place where the trees thin out into the meadow, the sun has gone down. Camilla has passed out small, solar-powered portable lights, and all seven of us kindergarteners are sitting on our benches in the open truck bed holding them. The kids are awed by being so far from the town at night. They speak to each other in whispers.

This is probably my thirtieth field trip to the landing site, but I feel it too. It's as unusual for me to be out this far as it is for them.

"I want to see the ship!" Kady says to me in a whisper-shout.

"There's no ship," I say. "The ship went back to where it came from."

"Why?"

"Because it was expensive and Daddy sold it to help pay for this." I wave my arm at the forest, the sky, everything. But of course Kady doesn't understand. Some of the adults who were born here don't care to think about the nature of our universe. How can I expect a five-year-old to get what I mean by a hand gesture? Next I'll try explaining that Daddy could have had another ship made out of thin air if he'd wanted to.

"I thought there was a spaceship," she says, peering over her lantern.

"Everyone, let's climb down. Careful now." Camilla glares up at me from her position at the bottom of the ramp leading down from the truck bed. For the last few minutes, I've been studiously ignoring her huffs and puffs as she wrangled the ramp into place. I shrug and smile at her. *What do you expect a little girl like me to do?* I say with my eyes.

The kids file down the ramp, stepping on each other's ankles. I wait and go last. Over time it's become second nature. When the kids are doing something fun, I try not to get in the way. It can be exhilarating to watch them experience all this for the first time. They have so much potential now. They could grow up to be the kind of people who want to explore our universe, who want to test its limits, who want to see how far we can go before the edges of the simulation dissolve. Or they could grow up to be like our teacher, plodding along year after year inside the world Daddy and his generation created.

I walk down the ramp with purpose, holding my head high, making as much impact with my tiny feet as I can. The kids aren't watching me, and Camilla doesn't have the spine to report to Daddy. All she cares about is that no one reports to him on her.

"Can you be helpful for once, Ella?"

"Are you going to teach them about how most of those stars up there will turn out to be illusions if we ever try to observe them up close?"

She doesn't humor me with an answer. Instead, she follows the kids into the meadow. They're waving their lanterns in each other's faces, attracting flies by the hundreds, sending bugs flying all around their heads.

"Eek, stop!" Jaden is chasing Kady around with two lanterns. She grabs one from another kid and waves it back in his face.

"Bugs to you!" she yells.

Jaden drops both lanterns and swats at the flies around his face.

Someone else has started crying.

I stand at the edge of the meadow, laughing. This has gone south faster than usual. Then again, I've never seen so many flies. It's probably related to the precipitous decline in the bird population. Which is no laughing matter, but I don't care right now. I'm having a night away from Daddy, and I'm going to enjoy it.

Camilla wades into the middle of the fray. "Okay, hand the lanterns over," she says. She walks around collecting them, and as she sets them down in a pile, she turns them off one by one. That has a magic effect on the kids, who finally sit on the grass and stay reasonably still. Camilla holds the last lantern.

"This is the spot where Philip Harkin first landed on Bella Inizio," she says. "The spaceship was only a little bit bigger than our schoolhouse, and he was all alone. And he was very brave, because very few people had traveled this far from Earth. And he was very strong, and that's why the people chose him to go and find a planet for them to live on."

Kady raises her hand high.

"Yes, Kady?"

"Is that Ella's daddy?"

"Yes, that's right," Camilla says, her voice strained.

All the kids turn to look at me. I'm standing with my arms folded and my feet planted. I hope they can't see my face in the darkness, because I can't bring myself to put on the mask right now. I'm fifty-eight years old, and I don't want to pretend to be five tonight. But I see the panic in Camilla's eyes, and I let my body relax. I unplant my feet and shift from one foot to the other.

"Ella, why aren't you with the group?" Camilla asks.

"I saw a rabbit!" I say, bounding over to the others and sitting at the end of the row.

"No you didn't," Jaden retorts.

"Yes I did!"

"Don't go running off again. We're all going to stay right here, okay?" Camilla pastes a smile on her face and goes on with her lesson.

"Sixty-six years ago, right at this time of night, right here, Philip Harkin landed his ship. And he stepped out into this meadow and saw what we're seeing right now." Camilla turns off her lantern and looks up.

My eyes are already acclimated to the darkness. I look up with the other kids. The moon is tiny, barely a pinprick, but the stars shine brightly across the sky. Despite myself, I get caught up. I see our sky through Daddy's eyes. I imagine what it must have been like to be all alone on a strange planet, the first human ever to set foot here, the first human ever to see these constellations. I breathe in the cool night air and imagine what it must have felt like for him to breathe it in for the first time.

Practically, there's no difference between what we're experiencing now and what Daddy felt. The simulation is as real to us as the planet was to Daddy. If I were suddenly sitting in the grass on the original

Bella Inizio, I'd never even know I'd been moved. I guess that's why they wait a few years to explain all that to the kids. For now, they just tell the story of Daddy's brave solo flight, the colonists' great migration, the founding of Harkin Town.

I wonder what the original looks like now, sixty-six years later. Time passes the same out there as in here. Are the buildings still standing, or has time and weather reduced them to ruins?

I look up at the stars knowing that even if Daddy ever lets me go, I'll never find what I'm looking for. I'll never see the real Bella Inizio. I'll never see Earth. I'll always be here, in this universe, rubbing up against the edges.

As Camilla continues telling the story, I shift on the grass so I can look behind me and to my left, to where the road continues along the meadow, out toward what's now a series of farms. I don't have to look far to see the spot where the servers are located on the real planet, where we actually are. Here there's nothing to mark the spot. But that's where he'll appear, or she, or they, or maybe it: the Technician who's due to stop by and check up on us, per Daddy's contract. Whoever comes will appear there, and he'll be the first person from outside ever to set foot in Bella Inizio.

I quickly go back to watching Camilla. If she knew what I want to do, she'd tell Daddy. And I don't blame her. After what he did to her, it wouldn't be fair for me to expect more.

"And now we all get to live here," Camilla finishes.

Kady raises her hand again. "Why was Earth bad?"

"Well, it wasn't bad," Camilla says, "but it was crowded. There were so many people that there were hardly any other animals or plants. They don't have forests like this one anymore." She gestures at the forest behind her, which spreads farther than the eye can see, even in daylight.

"Did everyone leave?"

"We don't know what happened after we left," Camilla says. "They might have gone to other planets."

Or continued the trend toward entering simulated universes and leaving their bodies to rot, I think. But of course, she isn't going to say that.

"Why don't we know?"

"We're going to have to talk about that some other time, Kady," Camilla says. "It's time to get home now. Everyone take a lantern, and no fighting, or we'll just ride home in the dark."

Wordlessly, I head for the pile of lanterns and help her hand them out to the kids. They manage not to be too unruly as we begin the short walk back to the truck.

"Stay together!" Camilla shouts after them as Jaden runs ahead. Of all of them, he's the most likely to get lost in the woods for a few hours.

"Don't you ever wonder what's happening in the real world?" I ask her.

"This is the real world, Ella," she says, sighing. "You're real and I'm real. All brains are just elaborate programs. What does it matter if ours are held in a server instead of a mass of flesh?"

"You're right, everything here is completely the same." I can't keep the bitterness out of my voice, especially now that we're about to get back in the truck and head home.

She stops short and looks down at me. "I'm sorry, Ella," she says. "I really am."

My stomach twists. "Don't be."

There's a long silence. She looks down at me, and I look up. She's seeing the face of a cute little five-year-old girl. I'm locking eyes with a woman who appears to be in her thirties, but is actually forty-seven. I'm older than she is by eleven years. And like every other adult on this planet, she knows it.

Kady tugs at my sleeve.

"What is it?"

"Ella, where's the truck?"

"What do you mean?" I don't know why she's asking me and not her teacher. Actually, I have a terrible idea of why. Kady's smart enough to understand that something's different about me. I need to do better around her. I need to make sure she doesn't act like this around Daddy.

"Oh my stars," Camilla says.

Kady and I follow her eyes. The other five kids are all standing where the truck used to be. The entire road is empty. There's no truck. And there's no way we missed somebody driving it away.

Camilla pulls her walkie-talkie out of its holster. "This is Camilla Wolkowitz," she says. "I've got my kindergarteners on a field trip to Day One Meadow? We're going to need another truck. I'm sorry, can you just send someone out? Yes, it's not operational. Okay, thank you." She carefully doesn't look at me as she returns the walkie-talkie to her belt. We both know what the missing truck means.

"Okay, let's gather in a circle!" Camilla says, making her voice as cheery as possible. "We're going to play a couple games before we go home!"

Kady stays next to me, and as the game begins, she takes my hand. The lanterns, now set on the ground in front of us, light up the kids' faces.

"Something's wrong," Kady says.

"It's all right," I say. "It's just a glitch. It can't hurt you."

But can it? She, and I, and all of us here, are elements of our universe, just like the truck. And so far, nothing that's gone missing has reappeared.

2

I DON'T KNOW if it's the disappearance of the truck or being out at night or the disquieting quiet of the last two kids waiting to be dropped off, but my mind turns to Samantha. I think about her a lot, but still she always seems to come out of nowhere. I'll be lying in bed, finally alone and able to give up the act, and I'll feel her presence next to me. It feels so real when that happens, as if she's sitting by the bed holding a picture book, her reddish-brown hair falling over one side of her face.

And she could appear, I think. It's possible, like so many things that will never happen.

I'm sitting in the dirt in the back yard, crying hysterically. The side of my face hurts where Daddy slapped me, and I don't understand. That's all I'm really thinking about. I don't understand why Daddy slapped me. What did I do?

Samantha sits down next to me. The scent of her lotion washes over me, fresh like the root it's made from, comforting. She puts an arm around me and pulls me close. "What happened, honey bunch?" she asks.

I try to stop myself from crying long enough to explain. The story comes out in short, heaving bursts. "When I grow up . . . and then. . . ." I press my hand to my face. "He hit me." I dissolve into sobs.

She pulls me closer. "I'm so sorry, Ella. I'm going to talk to him, okay? I'm going to make sure it doesn't happen again."

"Why!" I get out.

"It's not okay," she says. "What he did was wrong. But he did it because he's sad that you're growing up."

"He did it because of her!" I rub my eyes with the back of one hand, suddenly angry. Her. He always wants me to be like her, and I don't understand how. I don't know her. I can't see her. I can't copy her. I don't understand what he wants me to do.

She's silent for a while as she holds me close. I don't like it. It scares me. It means she doesn't know what to do either.

"Ella would never want this," she says finally. "Ella would have loved her little sister. Please don't blame her."

"What happened to her? Why isn't she here?" I know that she's gone, that a lot of people used to be here but aren't any more. I know that more people would have

been gone if Daddy hadn't done something, and somehow thanks to him, nobody will ever disappear again. But that doesn't explain it. How could somebody be gone?

"Before we came here, there was a disease," Samantha says. "That means something that hurts you from the inside. Don't worry, we don't have them anymore. But this disease, it made people feel really bad, and then. . . ." She pauses, and I know there's something she thinks I won't understand. She thinks I'm too young.

"I'm old enough," I say. "I'm seven."

"And then they died. They were gone. Ella was gone. And her mother—your mother—Vera Harkin, and many others." She wipes tears out of her eyes. "My son, his name was Davin. He was only a little older than Ella."

My heart leaps into my throat. A son? Was he someone she loved as much as me? Did she love him more than me?

"Are you going to make a new Davin?"

She shivers, and it takes her a moment. She speaks quietly. "No, I wouldn't. I don't know how. Only your Daddy knows how. But I wouldn't. Never." She stands up and takes a few steps away from me, wrapping her arms around herself.

That's when I realize how wrong I am. I understand that I was never supposed to exist.

"Ella, you have to go." Camilla's voice shakes me

from my memory. It's just the two of us on the truck now. I'm her last stop. Daddy's house is in the center of town, and we've wound our way around the edges, coming closer and closer this whole time.

I don't see Daddy, but I know he's there. He's standing just inside the doorway, looking out through the screen. I take a deep breath and gear myself up. It was so nice to be able to drop the act just for a few minutes, to be able to exist without trying to act five. But my breather is over now.

"Bye!" I say cheerily, waving my hand as I step down from the cab. I run around the back of the now-empty truck bed and make a beeline for the front door. I saw how tired the other kids were, but Daddy remembers that Ella had a lot of energy. Ella was cheerful. Ella never sulked or whined or cried.

The screen door opens toward me as I approach. Daddy steps outside, down the three steps, kneels down, and opens his arms. I run into them, and he lifts me into the air and spins me around.

I giggle and protest. "Daddy, stop!"

He stops and bounces me in his arms. "How was the field trip, pumpkin-head?"

"It was dark!" I say. "Did you really land there all by yourself?"

"Yes, I did!" He carries me inside and closes first the screen door and then the inner door with one hand. My heart speeds up, and I take a deep breath, then another. I imagine that I'm Kady coming home to her daddy. I imagine that this is really my first time going on that field trip. I put myself inside someone else's mind. Anybody's mind but mine.

Daddy sets me down. "I bet you're tired. I heard about your little problem with the truck. But first let's have your bedtime snack."

I *am* hungry. Camilla stopped bringing snacks on the field trip three years ago, when some mom's idea of fun sprinkle-covered cupcakes ended up all over the truck bed, the meadow, and the kids' clothes. But it's not like I have a choice. Daddy puts food in front of me, and I eat. So I sit at the kitchen table in my booster seat while Daddy spreads nut butter on thick crackers. Just as he's setting the plate in front of me, his walkie-talkie buzzes.

"Harkin." He smiles at me and watches while I take a bite. "Yes, I heard. That's not an element I have access to." He turns away from me, the way he always does when he's on the walkie-talkie. I don't know if he realizes he's doing it, but I think he's afraid that if I see the face he uses for adult stuff, he'll scare me. As if hitting me didn't.

My head tries to wrap around this for the millionth time. But I don't understand it. I never will. As long as I act the part, he loves me. When I stop, he doesn't. That's it.

I feel Samantha's presence behind me. I've read

that a lot of people used to feel the presence of the dead this way. Back when there was death. People used to imagine their loved ones with them. They'd imagine so hard that they'd believe it was true, so they made up ghosts and poltergeists, good spirits and bad ones. They imbued these spirits with their own guilt or their own hopes. I imagine that her hand touches my shoulder. *I loved you,* I imagine her saying.

I take a bite of my cracker.

I remember the screaming. Samantha's, and later, Daddy's. You would think that deleting a person would be painless, that there would be no sound at all. But you'd be wrong.

"There's a three-month window," Daddy says. "I know. I wanted it to coincide with the celebration, but that's how it works." He shakes his head, although there's no one to see. "No, it's all within expected parameters. The Technician will get your truck back. Or I'll make sure it takes top priority for fabrication. Goodnight to you too. And say hello to Radiance. Okay, goodbye." He clicks the button on the walkie-talkie and sets it on the counter. "Tough crowd, pumpkin," he says.

I continue eating, not daring to hope that he'll talk to me about the Technician.

"You can't have a universe without a few glitches, you know?"

I look up at him with big, trusting eyes.

"A man's going to come to make sure everything is working right," he says. "He'll bring the birds back to the forest. Return that truck. Heck, he'll even find all those socks gone missing." He chuckles to himself.

"Will he find Samantha?" I ask. I make my voice and eyes as innocent as possible. I don't care if he hits me. He always does it again eventually. Why shouldn't his next breakdown be tonight?

"Silly goose," Daddy says. He plucks my nose between his thumb and forefinger. "Samantha's not lost. She just joined the Western Settlement. She'll be back to visit any day now."

I think about pushing him, asking him why he won't let me see her letters, but I lose my nerve. Sometimes, when he hits me, it hurts a lot. Sometimes he breaks bones. We don't get sick like people used to, but we feel pain. We get injured. We take time to heal. I don't want to experience any more pain, and I hate myself for it.

"Can I go to bed now?" I ask.

"Sure, pumpkin-head. Let's get your teeth brushed." Daddy takes my now-empty plate and sets it in the sink. I get up from the table slowly. I'm tired. Bone tired, as if I was in the body of a fifty-eight year old woman. People used to complain about aging so much. Aches and pains and fat and fatigue. I'd give anything to feel it all. I'd give anything to have a body that would get older, reach its prime, and then begin to break down.

I follow Daddy into the bathroom to go through the ritual. It's what I have to do so he'll let me sleep.

3

WHY DO WE NEED SLEEP?

That one I can't blame on Daddy. The colonists were in agreement about what they wanted their lives to be like. They came to a beautiful, pristine, earthlike planet so they could build a community and live like their ancestors in the twentieth century. They fantasized about owning a planet that still had a robust natural world and modifying it to suit their needs.

Their ancestors had the opportunity to shape Earth in their own image; why shouldn't the colonists of Bella Inizio?

Too bad that Bella Inizio, like Earth, was deadly.

By the time more than three thousand of the original fifteen thousand colonists had died of a mysterious, incurable gastrointestinal disease, the survivors were ready to admit their mistake. They'd been wrong about wanting a real planet with all its pitfalls. What they really wanted, instead, was a world almost exactly like a real planet. What they wanted was a place where they could have everything they'd dreamed of but without disease, without aging past their thirties, without worrying about hardship and starvation and death.

So just like millions of people before them, they decided to ditch their bodies and upload themselves. Like those who came before, they made a contract with Clawhammer Corporation, one of the two big names in simulated-universe building. But some things about this contract were different. For Clawhammer, simulated universes were just one of many ways to earn a few gazillion bucks. Their original and still primary business was mining newly-accessible planets. And it turned out that Bella Inizio had some valuable deposits.

So the colonists of Bella Inizio made a trade: Clawhammer Corporation would build one of their premium simulated universes right here on the planet. They would image the planet and create as perfect a replica as possible, minus that pesky deadly disease. It would all be done to the colonists' specifications, as approved by the colony's founder, Phil Harkin, my daddy.

There was no need for anyone else to vet the contract. Sure, some of the others skimmed it, but with all that writing, who was going to scroll through every single boring word? Who was going to notice that deep in the fine print, Daddy had given himself powers that the other colonists hadn't agreed to?

Daddy, who as the homesteader technically owned the entire planet, signed the contract. Clawhammer gave him what he asked for.

Daddy is a morning person. He loves sunrises. When I was little, for real, we used to sit outside on the porch and have our breakfast. I have this vivid memory of the three of us sitting at that little wooden table: me, Daddy, and Samantha.

They sit close together, their mugs touching, steam rising from their tea into the cold air. I am wrapped in an oversized coat, slurping up my hot porridge sweetened with sugar root.

"I think I've found the solution," Daddy says.

Samantha doesn't answer him. She pulls her cup close to her, wraps her hands around it.

"You don't have to worry," Daddy says. "Vera will love you both the way I do."

"Phil. . . ." Samantha's voice trails off. She looks up at the sky, at the pure blue vista dotted with thin white clouds. I follow her gaze, and the porridge sticks in my mouth. I know something's wrong, but I

have no idea what it is. "Think about how she'll feel, living like that."

"Living like what?" Daddy turns to her, fork in hand, his eggs stabbed.

"You're talking about. . . ." Samantha looks at me and shakes her head.

"What?" I ask.

"Nothing, honey bunch," Samantha says. "Adult stuff."

After breakfast, they packed me off to kindergarten. The teacher was Mr. Perron then. A few years later, he really did move to the Western Settlement. Daddy and Samantha never explained to me what they were talking about, and so for a while I forgot about it. But I was a curious kid, and by the time I was seven years old, I already felt like I was constrained. I already wanted to be able to act older than Daddy wanted me to act. I already knew there was something different about me and the way I grew.

I knew I couldn't talk about what I'd do when I grew up, or Daddy would slap me. I knew that Daddy could do things other people's daddies couldn't, and I knew that most of what he did happened in a room with the door closed, the one I wasn't allowed to go into.

The night before I first snooped into what Daddy was doing, I saw Samantha leaving that room, and she was crying. She was bawling as badly as I cried

after Daddy slapped me. It was late, and I was supposed to be in bed.

"Why are you crying?" I asked her.

"Go back to bed," she said.

I stared up at her. I'd never seen her cry like this,
and it scared me. "What did he do?" I asked.

She put a hand on my back and ushered me back
to my bedroom. "Nothing, honey bunch. It's just his
work. Adult stuff."

Of course, that wasn't a satisfying answer. Why
did work have to be adult stuff? Why couldn't she tell
me the truth? I knew Daddy had to be doing something bad in there. I loved Daddy, but I knew that
he did bad things, and I knew he'd done something
bad to Samantha, and I had to know what it was.
So the next evening, after Daddy had gone into that
room and closed the door, I made a plan.

The attic was right above that room, and I knew
there were places in the attic where the boards had
holes. I was shaking as I opened the attic door and
climbed up the stairs, making sure to be as quiet as
possible. I slid through the boxes and piles of things.
I looked for light coming from below, and I found
it. I crawled onto my belly, and I peered down into
the room.

A woman was lying on the floor. She was completely naked, and she was on her back. It was like
she was sleeping, but people didn't sleep in that

position, with both legs straight out and both arms lying flat. I sat up straight in the dark attic. I was shivering, and I didn't know why. *It's just a lady,* I told myself. Slowly, I lowered myself back to the floor. I pressed my eye to the hole.

The woman's face was familiar. It was like mine. Looking at her was like looking into a funny mirror that changes you and makes you taller or fatter.

Things Daddy had said rushed through my mind. *She had eyes like yours. She loved French toast. She played the flute. She loved you.*

And when Samantha said, *think about how she'll feel.* Samantha had been telling Daddy not to do something, and that something was this.

The woman's eyes opened.

She looked up; I looked down.

She knew me. I knew her. I wanted to say *mother.* I choked on the word. Because she wasn't. I knew she wasn't. Daddy had also told me that my mother was gone. He'd made it sound like it was forever, like we had come here, to the house we lived in, and she didn't because she couldn't. Because *she was gone.*

I looked down, and she looked up.

Her eyes blinked. Her mouth moved. It opened and closed, but there was no sound.

I pressed my hand against the attic floor. The rough wood impressed lines into my fingers. Daddy had gone somewhere, and something was wrong, and she needed me.

Her mouth continued moving. Her chest heaved. Her arms and legs lay on the ground unmoving, heavy as logs.

Daddy would come back soon. I couldn't let him catch me, but I also couldn't leave this woman lying there. I had to help her. I slid back from my spot on the floor and scrambled down the steep stairs, and then I tiptoed around the corner to Daddy's office. Daddy had told me never to go in, and I had been too afraid of him to disobey, but the door wasn't locked. He must have thought fear would be good enough.

The woman was still lying there. I knelt down next to her, and she looked at me.

Her chest heaved. Her eyes blinked. Tears leaked from them, spilled over the edges of her eyes and down her cheek.

"Mother," I whispered.

Her mouth moved, but there was still no sound. One of her hands twitched, and I picked it up and held it in both of my hands. I didn't know what to do. I had no way to help her, and I couldn't call Daddy. I couldn't call Samantha, because she didn't want to see this. I knew in my bones that if she saw this, something terrible would happen.

"What should I do?" I asked her.

"Up," she said. At least, I thought that was the word that came from her lips, that floated through the air toward me, soft as her breath.

I let go of her hand and got behind her head. I put my hands under her shoulders, and she pressed both hands into the floor. I heaved. She lifted a hand and grabbed the desk. Her fingers were pink and soft. She had almost no fingernails. All of her skin was unmarked and new. Her hair was only an inch long, and her face was exposed as she sat all the way up with a loud gasp.

I leaned into her back, afraid she'd fall. One of her hands gripped the desk until the knuckles were white, and the hand on the ground pressed and relaxed, pressed and relaxed, as though she couldn't hold it steady.

She was falling back into me. Her breath heaved, her fingers grasped, her legs twitched, and she was heavy. I tried to hold her, but as she fell she pushed me back. My legs scrambled against the ground, but she was too much, and she kept falling, and I let her go as slowly as I could, but a few inches from the ground, I had to let her drop.

Her head hit the floor, and her arm fell, and her legs moved. They kicked, suddenly full of energy. *Kick kick, twitch. Kick.* Her mouth opened and closed.

"I'm sorry," I said. "I can't hold you up."

Her legs stopped moving, and slowly, her pink arm reached up. Her hand touched my cheek. Tears continued to pour from her eyes.

"Ella," she said.

Or did she? Maybe she just made a sound. Maybe she had no idea who she was or who I was.

"Oh no." Samantha grabbed me from behind. With her arms around my waist, she pulled me away. She spun me toward her, away from the woman on the ground. "Oh, Ella." She held me close to her.

"Mother!" I yelled. I pressed my face into Samantha's stomach. "Mother, Mother, Mother." I was sobbing, and I wasn't sure why. I wasn't sure what I'd seen. A woman with pink skin, a woman who knew me, a woman who couldn't move right and couldn't speak. A woman who was wrong. Like I was wrong. "She's like me. She's like me. Like me," I repeated.

"No. Ella, no." Samantha pressed her hand against my hair. "She's sick. Remember I explained sick? It won't happen to you. She's different from you."

"She's my mother."

"No, she's not your mother." Samantha got down on her knees and kept one hand on my head. "I'm your mother. Ella, I'm your mother. I love you. I will always be here for you. I promise." She wiped a tear from her eyes. "It's me. I'm your mother. Not her."

I nodded. I knew what she meant, and I knew it was true, but I also knew it was a lie. I started to turn my head, but Samantha pulled me back to her. "We're going to go now. We're going to leave this room, okay?"

"Okay." I didn't want to see the woman again. I didn't want to see her mouth opening and closing and her feet trying to kick and her hands trying to grasp. But as Samantha pulled me through the door, I did manage to look back. I caught one last glimpse of my mother lying there on the floor, naked and pink. One hand fluttered, as if she was reaching for something. And then Samantha slammed the door behind us.

The next morning, she was gone.

Looking back on it, I know that if she saw me at all, it's unlikely that she recognized me. It's possible that she didn't even see me, that I projected my feelings onto her. But I think that a human brain, even one as muddled and damaged as hers must have been, is still capable of a lot of things. Maybe a mother can know a daughter from the slightest of inputs. I think she opened her eyes and saw a little girl she knew to be Ella. And I saw a woman who meant something to me.

Maybe, if you're human, any woman lying on the ground, naked and hurting, would mean something. Maybe I saw another human being in distress, and so I felt a bond with her. Maybe I recognized that this was Vera, and everything I'd heard crystalized in my mind. Or maybe she *was* my mother because Daddy used her genetic profile in the program that created me. Maybe no matter how strange your existence is, you know your mother when you see her.

She was Daddy's first attempt at Vera, but there have been many others. Now, when I see her, I know better than to watch. I don't wait to find out if her eyes will open. I leave the attic, and I wait until she's gone again. Because she's always gone again, eventually. Daddy keeps trying, but he will never succeed.

Recreating dead people from brain scans, no matter how good the scans are, just isn't possible. There are two ways to add a person to a universe: You can upload her directly, by attaching a bunch of thingies to her head and moving her into the universe in the blink of an eye, thereby capturing the exact quantum states of every single data point in her physical brain. Or, you can create an embryo inside the program that will grow and learn and develop like any human without ever having a body in the physical world.

Clawhammer created our universe so that women can get pregnant and have the experience of giving birth, complete with pain. Everyone younger than Daddy's generation was born this way, except for me. Daddy told the computer to create me, and it did. I started with a tiny little bunch of cells just like any physical human, but I was never inside a woman.

Daddy grew me in the very same room where he made Vera. He told the computer to make me look exactly like Ella, but he couldn't make me *be* Ella. He couldn't have done that even if he'd had her scanned. I'm my own person, just like every other unique human being ever born.

Vera, Ella's mother, was unique too, and it's not possible to bring her back.

But Daddy doesn't believe there's anything he can't do or anything he can't have. He's kept trying for all these years, and he'll keep trying until someone stops him.

4

Now, AGE FIFTY-EIGHT, still fitting into the same small space on the attic floor, I lie still while Daddy works. I watch what he does. I watch how he enters the system. I memorize his gestures. I read the display, and I see how he gets from one place to another. After all this time, I no longer pay attention to how he manipulates Vera's brain scans. But there are other things he works at.

I've learned that Daddy doesn't have access to all the elements of our universe. He can't create a kitchen table out of thin air or make a truck disappear. That stuff isn't in the contract. He only demanded control over one type of element: people. Daddy can go into the computer and isolate the element that is you or your husband or your daughter, and he can delete you, or them. He searches for the code that represents the person, and if it's a baby he wants to delete, he finds and isolates the new code that's nested within.

I've watched several times as he's held two fingers against the tendrils of the interface and swiped them half an inch to the left. And then the baby or the woman or the loved one is gone.

That's not the only thing I've learned. I know that servers on the real, physical planet hold us in their cold metal boxes. I know that there are smaller boxes that could hold the code for a person and that those boxes could be physically moved through space. In that way, a person could be moved from one simulated universe to another. I don't know enough, and I never will. But I have to be ready to take my chance.

Now, I watch Daddy's gestures to see if he does anything that will clue me in to exactly when Clawhammer's Technician will be here. I know it's supposed to be sometime in the next few months. But will he or she or they or it appear with no warning, or will we know the day before, the morning of? Will I have enough time to plan anything?

Daddy leans back in his chair, and that's my cue. Slowly, carefully, as quietly as no one, I slide back from my hole. I tiptoe down the stairs and slip back into my bedroom and under the covers. I slow my heartbeat and my breathing. I calm my mind and my senses, and outwardly, I become a child asleep.

But instead of sleeping, I think about Camilla Wolkowitz. I remember the night eight years ago when she showed up at our door, when I learned what he took from her and why.

I was in my bedroom wearing my pajamas. I didn't want to go to bed. *I shouldn't have to go to bed,* I kept thinking. *I'm fifty years old,* I thought. *I should be able to go for a walk. I shouldn't be afraid to leave my bedroom.* My mind raced on all the things I should do, all the ways I should defy Daddy.

He can't delete everyone, I thought. I stood with my hand on the doorknob. *He won't delete me. What can he do to me that he hasn't already done?* But I remembered Samantha, and I was afraid. I remembered what it was like to feel pain, and I was frozen in place.

Bang bang bang. Someone was pounding on the door to the street.

My hand on the doorknob was slick with sweat.

"Phil Harkin, open this door!" Camilla's voice stormed the house. *Bang bang bang.* "You open this fucking door right now!" *Bang bang bang. Bang bang bang.* "I don't give a fuck, Phil! I Do. Not. Give. A. Fuck." *Bang bang—*

"My daughter is asleep," Daddy said. His voice was quiet, but it shot back to me.

"Your daughter is an adult," Camilla said. "She shouldn't be in bed at twenty hours."

"You're here because you want something," Daddy said. "What is it?"

"Don't pretend you don't know, Phil." Camilla's voice changed like a switch had been flipped. Pleading now.

"I don't have anything for you, Camilla. You made your decision."

"What decision did I make?" Her voice cracks, rises. "What did I do to deserve this? What did I do for *Darius* to deserve this? For *Francine* to deserve this?"

"If you didn't know that, you wouldn't blame me. Go back home, Camilla. Live your life. It's my gift to you."

I leaned my ear against the door. All I could hear was Camilla sobbing. But I knew Daddy was still out there. His presence loomed over her. I pictured him standing in the doorway, peering down at her, one hand on the door as if ready to slam it in her crumpled face.

"Everything you teach in that school needs to be appropriate for children, Camilla," Daddy said. "Do you understand?"

I listened and listened, but Camilla didn't say another word. Daddy didn't say another word. Wind rattled the door. A breeze wound its way through the house. Cold air slid through the cracks around my bedroom door. Finally, I heard the sound of a door closing with a soft click, and the wind died. The cold remained. My hand slipped on the sweat on the doorknob and fell to my side.

Camilla had given me some books. Adult stuff. She said they were classics. She said I could read them while she taught the other kids, and it would be our secret. Inside one of these books was a device that had other books on it, and documents, and all sorts of things that taught me about the world we live in. For fifteen years, I read everything I could. And I kept our secret. I never told another soul.

Somehow, Daddy must have found out. Maybe he saw me with the reader one day when he picked me up from school. Maybe I said something that showed him that I knew more than I was supposed to know. As I stood there behind my closed door, I realized that I had to have given myself away. How could I have read all of those books and articles and documents without the knowledge changing how I behaved? I hadn't told Daddy that Camilla had helped me, but I had betrayed her just the same.

I was the reason Daddy had deleted Darius, Camilla's husband. And Francine—that must have been the name of her unborn child. Everyone had seen the bump. She had been so happy to become a mother.

I didn't leave my room that night after all. I didn't sleep. I couldn't cry. I wanted to wish I'd never read anything, never learned more than I was supposed to, but I found that I couldn't. I found that I didn't want to go back and change anything, and I hated myself. I was selfish, and I was worthless, and I had destroyed Camilla's life.

Now, I lie awake in bed with my eyes closed, slowing my breathing. I wonder if Camilla's husband and baby still exist somewhere, or if when Daddy deleted them, they were lost forever. Is there a backup server somewhere where the deleted go? Where babies Daddy stole from their mothers' wombs might grow up? Where Samantha is waiting for me?

I open my eyes. Light filters in from beneath the door.

I feel the weight of my head making an indent in the pillow. Is it possible that the real world actually feels different, and everything Daddy and the others have said about living there is a lie? Is it possible that there is no real world, and no Technician, and no other universes for my program to move to?

If I thought there was truly no way out, I know what I'd do.

But I'm not ready yet. I'm going to talk to the Technician when he or she or they or it comes. I'm going to find a way out of here.

5

You'd think after all these years I'd forget some things about Samantha. Maybe the sound of her voice would fade and I wouldn't hear her every time a woman laughs. Or maybe I'd forget the exact color of her hair, and I'd stop comparing it to every redhead I see. *Samantha's hair had more brown. Samantha's hair was thicker. Samantha's hair had more wave to it.*

Maybe I'd stop thinking about her feet, clad in slippers, padding down the hallway toward my room. But when Daddy walks, even in his stocking feet, he walks heavy. He opens my bedroom door with too much force. His deep voice reverberates about, disturbing my eardrums, shaking me awake.

I must have fallen asleep again in the early hours of the morning. I'd like to stay in bed now. It's Rest Day, after all: the day the colonists of Bella Inizio added to Earth's week to make up for the planet's cycle. Saturday, Sunday, Rest Day. But little children never get to choose the hours they spend in bed. They can't go to bed late or sleep in. They can't get up early without being chastised.

"Good morning, sunshine," Daddy says, a big smile on his face. "Don't forget you have a play date with Kady this morning."

"Oh yeah," I say, sitting up. Kady, who's too smart for her own good and has figured out that I'm different somehow.

A few minutes later I'm sitting at the breakfast table waiting for Daddy to finish making pancakes. The pancakes are a Rest Day tradition. He makes them in different shapes. I think they're supposed to be characters from some entertainment thing that Daddy and his generation had back on Earth. Samantha used to tell me the stories, but they blend together in my mind.

She said you would put thingies on your head and go into a place that was like a universe except it wasn't just regular people who lived there. There were also these characters, and they made you help them do things, and it was supposed to be fun, but I still don't understand how. I like reading books, but you can put a book down. Nobody in a book ever made you help them do things.

I eat my pancakes with a smile on my face.

Funny how last night when I was with Camilla and the kids at Day One Meadow I barely thought about what Daddy did to her. I spend every weekday with her, and I almost never think about it. It's only when I'm not with her, at random times, when I least expect to hear her voice, that the pounding on the door breaks through my thoughts.

She tried to help me, and she paid for it. She tried to tell Daddy he was doing something wrong.

Anyone who helps me get away will pay. But Clawhammer's Technician will be outside our system. Daddy won't be able to hurt him. Will he?

I don't want to eat any more and yet I do. Most kids are hungry because they're growing. You put food into your body, and your body turns it into muscle and bone. But the food that goes into my body goes nowhere. I don't understand it. Daddy makes me eat like an ordinary child, so I should have rolls of fat by now. But whatever has stopped my growth has prevented any sign that my size isn't normal.

At least, if I go play with Kady, I'll be out of this house. I'll be under the watchful eye of Kady's mother, Briana, who knows the limits of my freedom. But still. At least Briana doesn't pretend she doesn't know.

I finish all the pancakes Daddy has given me, and I drink down a glass of nocta juice. The nocta grow wild not far from here. They taste like sweet cranberries, Daddy says. On another field trip, Camilla takes us all to the bog where they grow, and we fish them out and eat them raw. That's one I look forward to, because I can't go there on my own. I can't experience wild berries unless I'm with an adult, and Daddy is so busy being in charge of things that he doesn't take me there often.

"Time to brush your teeth, sweetie," Daddy says.

I brush them. No one's teeth get all that bad here. They won't get so diseased that they all fall out. But if you don't take care of them, they'll hurt. Always, things that won't kill us cause us pain, and that was a choice. Daddy and his friends could have chosen a universe where no one felt pain at all, where it was impossible to break a bone, where you wouldn't feel cold or heat or blunt force trauma. But they believed that life requires pain, that to exist without hurting is no existence at all, that there is something fundamentally good about human suffering.

I read a lot about the old religions during those years before Daddy figured out what Camilla had done. It would have made sense for real twentieth-century people to have used their supernatural beliefs to justify making people suffer. But Daddy and the other colonists aren't religious. They don't believe in a god that wants them to suffer. They just believe that suffering is natural, and natural is morally good.

Except of course, death. That was a natural bridge too far.

I also read an article about the prevalence of simulated universes. It said that ninety percent of the universes Clawhammer builds for young customers are like ours. It's only the old, who wait to upload themselves until they're near death, who ask for universes that are painless. The old have lived through enough pain, the writer said. The young have yet to understand.

Daddy helps me put on my jacket, and then he takes me by the hand. We walk out into the morning air, and the sun is bright, and I try to ignore the hand in mine and what it means, and I breathe in the crispness.

Bella Inizio is a beautiful planet. It's much more beautiful than Earth, which was built up with cities and had hardly any trees and birds and things when Daddy and the others left it. As soon as people found out how to fold space, they abandoned Earth by the thousands and hundred-thousands. Those who stayed behind were more likely to upload themselves than ever.

And now? No one living on Bella Inizio knows for sure, but it's possible there's hardly anybody there now, except inside the simulations. It's possible it's all Clawhammer Technicians and machinery run by AIs. It's possible they stopped leaving too. It's possible they've destroyed their universes, killing everybody inside them. It's possible an asteroid destroyed the whole planet. Nobody knows and nobody can know.

If we built a spaceship and went to Earth, we'd find that our simulation doesn't have that information. Earth would have taken a lot of extra work to simulate. So if we went there, we'd find a planet with rudimentary nature. We'd find a place we could live on but with none of our history.

A bird chirps to our left.

"Oh, that's good," Daddy says. "Ella, did you hear the bird?"

"Yes. Shouldn't there be more?" I ask.

"Yes, there should be. Nature needs a little tune-up. But I'll tell you a secret. Do you promise not to tell your little friend?"

"I won't tell." The bird is still chirping in the background. It sounds frantic. Maybe it's searching for a mate that disappeared into thin air.

"The birds will be back soon," Daddy says. "It could even be later today."

"Today? How?" My heart is beating in my chest. Can he possibly mean what I think he means?

"I got a message this morning. Just a little beacon saying the Technician's coming." Daddy points to the road that leads out of town, the same one we drove up last night. "Someone will be coming from there."

"How can they bring back the birds?" I ask. What I want to know is, will they bring back the same birds, or will they create new birds? Are the birds that disappeared somewhere else? But Daddy will know what I mean if I ask that.

"Well, I don't know how, but this person will. He'll be coming to take care of us."

"So we won't lose any more trucks?"

Daddy laughs. "That's right. We won't lose any more trucks."

But what about people? I have to clamp my mouth shut not to ask that. I'm not aware of any people who have disappeared on their own like the truck and the birds. People only disappear when Daddy makes them. He must know I know that. I was there when he deleted Samantha. I heard her screaming. How could he truly believe that with all that noise, I wouldn't hear?

But he tells me she's in the Western Settlement. He tells me about letters she sends to us. What a great time she's having exploring the frontier. How much she misses us, but how difficult it is to travel back.

He makes her sound like the kind of bird that's just flown away.

6

"THAT'S KADY'S HOUSE," I say, just to say something. Her house is at the edge of town. Her parents grow vegetables on the farm that stretches out behind it. It started out as a small garden, but they kept growing it. Now it feeds a lot of people. Kady's mom used to work for Daddy, taking care of his schedule. But now she's able to farm full time.

Daddy knocks on the door, and Kady's mom, Briana, answers. She smiles pleasantly.

"Well, hello! Chilly this morning, isn't it?"

"Should be getting warmer soon," Daddy says.

"Boy, I sure hope so. Last year we had that late freeze." She shakes her head, pretending to remember the lost crops. Most people who talk to Daddy are pretending about something.

"Forecast is good," Daddy says. "Of course, you never can tell with the weather."

"I'll walk Ella back after lunch," Briana says.

"Fine, fine."

"Don't forget, it's Rest Day. Wouldn't want to catch you working." Briana shakes her finger playfully.

"Perish the thought." Daddy winks at her and turns around. Briana and I both watch until he reaches the end of the block, and then she puts a hand on my back and ushers me inside. As soon as she closes the door, her smile fades.

"How are you doing, Ella?" she asks.

I search the room behind her for Kady.

"It's okay, Kady's out back."

"I'm fine," I say. I want to tell someone about my plan, and I know Briana wants to help me. But that's exactly why I can't tell her. It wouldn't be fair to put her entire family at risk for me.

"You can stay past lunch if you want. I just said that because we talked about it earlier. I'll say the two of you are having a great time."

"Thank you," I say.

Briana pulls something out of her pocket. "I'll give you a warning before Kady's ready to play." She puts it in my hand, and I see that it's a book reader like the one Camilla let me use at school. Not quite from the time period they're trying to emulate, but not too far off either. Close enough for the colonists.

"I can't," I say. "It's not safe."

Briana puts her hand on my back again, like I'm a

child, and leads me down a hallway. "It's just you and me in the house right now. Nagesh won't be back until later." She pushes me into Kady's bedroom. There's a small bed covered by a pink bedspread with black flowers on it. A pile of rag doll animals lies on top of it. One corner of the room is strewn with carved wooden figures: a horse, a cow, a Bella-bear, a woman.

Briana closes the door behind me and leaves me alone.

I turn on the device. *Understanding the Maintenance of Your New Universe* appears on the screen. I quickly flip through it. It's an article about Clawhammer's maintenance program, including how often the Technicians will come and what they will do. I read the article as fast as I can. The whole time I feel guilty about what Briana's doing for me. And I wonder how she knows that I've been planning something. But maybe she doesn't know. Maybe she's trying to give me the idea.

Once every sixty years. Teams of two.

. . . if any issues are identified, your Technicians will remain on site until a resolution is achieved.

. . . your Technicians are not authorized to make any modifications to the parameters of the universe or to the contract.

. . . movement of sentient elements requires an additional fee.

My heart leaps. Never mind the fee. Movement is contemplated. It's a thing that the Technicians can do. I'm not delusional to hope that they might be able to help me. I keep reading all the way to the end of the article. There's another article after that. *Troubleshooting from Inside: A Manual for Those with Elemental Control.*

"Holy shit," I whisper to myself. This has stuff about how to access the servers, if you have the proper permissions. Daddy doesn't have permissions to do most of the stuff they talk about here. But I suck it up. I read so quickly that I'm afraid I'll stuff my brain and miss something. A lot of it I've figured out, but this gives details. This is more than I could have hoped to learn just by watching. And I have to remember it all, every detail.

I know this is the one and only time I'll ever be able to see this document. But it's all for the layperson, for people who don't know anything about programming a universe. It just talks about how to use the in-universe interface to do basic things.

I'm elated. My heart is beating a million times a minute. But at the same time, I want to cry. Because this isn't enough. Because I can never hope to learn enough from reading this manual or even from reading the entire database of material that the colonists had uploaded with them.

Knock knock. "Ella, honey, Kady is going to have

a snack. Would you like to join us?" Briana comes into the room without waiting for me to answer. She takes the device from me, slips it into her pocket, and presses her hand to my back. "I've baked some crisp crackers with sugar root for you."

"Thank you," I say. I smile up at her like a five-year-old. I have to get in the groove before I see Kady, because she's too smart. I don't know whether Daddy will forgive her for getting out of line just because she's a little kid. I don't know of any kids who disappeared after they were born. Maybe even Daddy wouldn't do that to someone. But I don't know that. I can't act like I believe Daddy has any limits. "But don't help," I blurt, just as we reach the door. "It's not safe."

"We made this universe too safe," Briana says. She looks down at me with a thin smile, and even though her face is like that of a woman in her thirties, there's an age to it. If you look closely, you can see it in all of the original colonists. You can see that the experience of life works changes on a person's face that no anti-aging program can entirely stop.

I remember that Briana's first husband and three children all died of the disease. And what led her to make the decision to leave Earth? I wish I could ask her, have a real conversation. In this moment I'm so desperate to ask, to talk, to know, that I almost do it. I almost pull her back into the room and talk to her as if we're two adult women.

But Briana pushes me through the door, and the moment is lost. We reach the kitchen, where Kady is sitting in front of a plate of crackers. They're fresh from the oven, still hot. I can smell the cinnamon from here and almost taste the sugar root.

"Hi, Ella!" Kady says. She's bouncing in her chair. "Mom said I had to wait until you got here."

"And you did it," Briana says. A real smile spreads across her face. "Was that so hard?"

"Yes!" Kady reaches for a cracker, and I sit down next to her at the little table and grab one for myself. I take a bite and close my eyes. It's heavenly. Nobody makes ordinary things like Briana. She's a wizard with her sugar root, with the Bella-adapted wheat that comes from miles out beyond the city, with the electric oven. And I also feel the something added, the ingredient that doesn't come from a farm. These crackers are baked with a mother's love. I understand somehow that if I were an adult, these crackers wouldn't taste half so good.

We eat the crackers quickly, leaving crumbs on the plate.

"Dad fixed the swings," Kady says. "Do you want to?"

"Not tired of that yet?" Briana asks.

"No! Come on!" Kady waves me toward the back of the house, and I follow her as she races out the back door and into the yard. It's a patch of natural grass with two large trees. One of them has nice strong branches, from which two swings hang. We each climb into one, and I push off with my feet.

"Bet you I can touch the clouds," Kady says, whooshing into the air.

"Bet *I* can," I say. I fly up, but it's not far enough, so I push myself back and forward again. I go higher. The clouds, of course, are high up in the sky, floating through the air, barely making a dent against the bright sun. They say the sun here is brighter than it was on Earth, but I wouldn't know. To me, this sun is normal.

This is the kind of sun that makes you believe you can do anything. When it's out and radiating its energy, it feels like I could reach the clouds by scrambling my little feet against the grass, as if I could let go of the seat of the swing and fly above and beyond the city. Maybe I could even fly to the Western Settlement.

A door slams inside the house. A man's voice. Noise. More voices? I try to figure out where they're coming from. I swing back and forth, back and forth, slowing down. For a minute there, I was a kid again. For a minute, I was enjoying myself. The thought suddenly crosses my mind that if I do escape, if I do manage to grow up, I have to remember to be a kid sometimes. I have to choose to swing until I reach the clouds or to taste the love a cracker is baked with.

Kady leaps off her swing and runs inside the house, so I follow. I like running because it's doing something. As we get inside the house, Kady's dad opens the front door again. There are people out there, a whole bunch of them.

"What's going on?" Kady asks.

"I don't know," Briana says.

"I want to see." Kady pushes past her mother and slips under her father's arm. I follow her. We stand together in the doorway and watch the crowd of people gathering. They're heading by us as if they're going to take the road out of town.

My heart leaps and my stomach does somersaults. Because I can only think of one reason why everyone would be so excited to go down that road at once.

"I want to see too!" I say. I bounce on my little five-year-old feet. I want to look up at Briana, to signal her, but I can't do that. I have to trust that she understands.

"All right, let's go out," Briana says. "You have to promise to stay with me though." She slips between Kady and me and takes one of each of our hands.

"I don't know," Kady's dad says.

"Oh come on, Nagesh, they're excited, not rioting."

Nagesh shakes his head. "Right. This is Bella Inizio. Everything's fine."

"Yes, it is." A look passes between them that makes me wonder. What happened to them on Earth? Why are they here? What stories do all of the original colonists have that no one has ever told me? "Okay, girls. Let's see what's happening."

7

WE JOIN THE CROWD, which is getting larger. There must be hundreds of people on the street now. My heart is trying to escape from my chest, and I'm hearing what I want to hear, what I wasn't sure I'd ever hear.

The Technician, people are saying.

He appeared.

A man.

Just one man?

A human?

Yes, a human man. Just one. He's coming.

Will I get my tractor back?

What about my lost socks?

Socks? A man laughs.

All my socks! a woman retorts.

People talk about their lost things: *elements*, I realize. A single sock probably wouldn't disappear. That lady's socks were probably programmed as a unit. As in, *woman gets entire drawer full of socks to warm her feet*, just like that drawer full of socks she had in her house on the original planet. I don't hear anyone mentioning people, even though I recognize a couple whose baby Daddy deleted. There must be others here who he's taken someone from, but the *talk* is about things. There's an anxiety in the group though. It hangs over all of us.

What if this man can't fix things? What if elements keep disappearing? What if the universe begins falling apart?

This man is like the old God. Everything is in his hands, and I don't like that. No one should have that much power. Not Daddy, not the Technician, not anyone.

Speaking of Daddy, there he is. He's walking quickly, passing on the left shoulder of the road, getting ahead of the other colonists. I have the urge to run to him because he's going to get to the Technician first. He'll be able to talk to the man, and that's how I can meet him. But Briana holds my hand firmly.

"We'll get there," she says.

She's right—Daddy can prevent me from talking to the Technician. But can Briana meet him at all? This is my only chance. I need her to help me or get out of my way. And I can't live with what might happen to her if she helps me.

With a hard jerk, I free myself from her hand. I run. I wind my way around people and push my way forward. It helps to be small to get around people. I risk getting trampled, but that's okay. What's the worst that could happen? I can't die. My element won't disappear. I might get stepped on. I might hurt. I might spend months in the hospital recovering. But none of that will matter if I can't get to the front of this mob, if I can't meet the Technician.

Briana's voice rings out from behind me. She must be calling my name, but I can't hear what she's saying. Other people call out for me. A man grabs me, and I squirm free. I head for Daddy. I call out for him. "Daddy! Daddy! Daddy!" People hear me say that, and they part. The whole mob slows and almost stops while they wait for me to slip through the spaces. "Daddy!"

Daddy sees me and stops. He holds out his hand, and I run to him. I grab his hand as tightly as I can.

"Briana was holding my hand, but I got away. Don't be mad at her," I say.

"You shouldn't have run, but I'm glad you found me," Daddy says. "Now let's move quickly." He doesn't have time to be mad at Briana or at me. He needs to see the Technician too. He needs to get there first, and I'm not sure why. Maybe just because he's the leader. Maybe because there's something he needs. My sweat turns cold as I realize that he probably wants Vera. But the Technician won't be able to help him. And what will happen when he gets told no?

We push forward, and the voices swirl around me. I can't hear what they're saying anymore. My hand is sweaty and so is Daddy's, and even though we're gripping each other as hard as we can, it feels like we're in danger of sliding away from each other. But I can't slide away from him. Not yet.

Up ahead of us, I catch a glimpse of dark red hair.

You can do this, Ella, I hear a voice say.

No, I can't, I reply.

Yes, you can.

It's impossible.

In the universe we live in, anything that can be imagined is possible.

She sounds so real that I almost break away from Daddy and run. But I know the woman up ahead of us is not Samantha. I know what I'm hearing is just things she's said to me before or that she *would* say. She would want me to find a way out of here.

She told me once that even though Clawhammer programmed our universe a certain way, other ways are still possible. Programming can be changed. You *could* drop a rock from your hand and have it fall up. You *could* step off the edge of the platform over the lake and instead of diving down into the water, find that you are flying into the sky. If I had access to the program, and the right skills, I could program anything. She was trying to tell me that I could grow, that there was a way.

She tried to tell Daddy.

I'll take her, Phil, she said.

What?

I'll go to the Western Settlement, and I'll take her. At least if she's with me, she can live a more normal life. If you won't let her grow, at least that's better.

I can't make her grow, Daddy said. *I don't have access to her parameters.*

There was a silence. Samantha wasn't prepared for that answer. Neither was I. Behind the kitchen door, I put my hands over my mouth. It had never occurred to me that Daddy couldn't change me if he wanted to.

What do you mean you don't have—

I said I don't, Sam.

Okay, but you don't have to keep making her act like—

It's not acting, Daddy said. *My Ella is a sweet girl. She was always that way.*

Phil, she's sweet. She's also eleven years old now. You have to treat her like the age she is.

Daddy started moving toward the door, and I had to move then. I had to go back to bed.

Now, at the edge of the crush of bodies, I listen for her voice. I strain my ears to hear words that she never spoke to me, that I just made up in my own head. I know she would tell me to keep going, to keep trying, to do whatever it takes, to hope.

But it's so hard, I tell her. My grip on Daddy's hand falters. Our hands slip and slide with our sweat.

The crowd suddenly becomes louder.

There he is!

Hello!

The Technician!

Where?

Move out of my way!

"Let us through!" Daddy bellows. We rush past the last few rows of people. The row in the very front has stopped. They're all mesmerized by what they see ahead of them. Daddy stops at the end of the first row, and we both stare.

A man is walking toward us. He's about the same height as Daddy, which is not too tall and not too short. His skin is pale like Daddy's. He's wearing a suit that's colored orange, and it's like the pictures Camilla showed us of men in the olden days when they went to space. It makes him shapeless, and yet somehow it also shows that he's fit. He's wearing heavy boots, and he walks toward us with purpose. In one arm he carries a helmet, and his short hair is messy as if he's just been wearing it. The hair sticks up all over the place, and there are also patches of it that are depressed, as if there's been something sticking to those spots. Which there would have been, I think, if he's temporarily uploaded himself.

He's planning to go out again, I think with a thrill. *It's possible it's possible it's possible.* Somewhere, this man has a flesh and blood body.

As he comes closer, I can see that he has stubble on his face. It's been a day or two since he's shaved. He's also sweating. Like any of us. Like a human being. He stops a few feet in front of us.

"Well, I see there's a welcoming committee." His voice is deep and smooth. It's the kind of voice you want to listen to.

Be a child, Samantha tells me.

I'm already acting like one. Without realizing it, I've moved behind Daddy's leg. I poke my head out and look up at the man.

"Are you a spaceman?" I ask.

"No, I'm just a Technician. I did come on a spaceship though."

"Then you *are* a spaceman!"

He laughs. "I guess so. It's not too different from riding in a. . . ." He raises an eyebrow. "You have cars? Like twentieth-century?"

Daddy clears his throat. "We have cars," he says.

"Well, it's like riding in a car," the man says, smiling down at me. "You get in, you have a ride, and you get out somewhere else."

I hide behind Daddy's leg again, heart beating wildly. I have to gauge how much I can say without making Daddy suspicious. Sometimes I think Daddy truly believes I'm still five years old. But at the same time, he *knows* I'm not. Otherwise, why would he get so angry?

"This is my daughter, Ella," Daddy says, smiling.

"Hello, Ella," the man says. "It's very nice to meet you." He pauses, stands up straight, and raises his voice. "My name is Niclaus. I'm one of the Technicians from Clawhammer. My buddy and I came along to make sure everything's working right. I just need people to report anything unusual."

The mob of people, previously so eager, is quiet. They stare at Niclaus as if he's a space alien rather than a man wearing what looks like a spacesuit. People look at each other. Some whisper.

A woman raises her hand. "Um, my socks disappeared."

Everyone laughs.

"Not like one sock," she protests, elbowing her neighbor in the ribs. "An entire drawer. One day they were there, and poof, gone the next."

More laughter.

"That could be an issue," Niclaus says. "Better that I talk to whoever's in charge here so I can get your reports in an orderly manner."

Daddy steps forward, pulling me with him. "Phil Harkin," he says, holding out his hand to shake.

"Oh, you're the founder," Niclaus says, clasping Daddy's hand. I feel a million miles below the two men.

"Yep," Daddy says. "Came here in a tiny ship, barely big enough to hold its AI and me. It took all of our resources and then some to afford it, but I got here first, staked our claim. After that, Clawhammer was willing to fund our transport. We were just going to give them some mining rights." Daddy's face is grim while he says this. It jolts me. I've always known that bad things happened to Daddy. But I've never thought about the depth of the failure.

Daddy never wanted to live in a simulation, I realize. He's here because he wanted to create me. Because he wanted Ella back. If not for her, and maybe for Vera, he would have left Bella Inizio behind.

"Nice to meet you," Niclaus says. "It's an honor. I don't meet a lot of homesteaders in my job. It's mostly Earth-based universes. Well, a lot of pockets out in the colonies."

"No other comprehensive set-ups on other planets?"

"Well, I won't say none," Niclaus replies. "I haven't

been assigned any. But I'm just a Technician. What all Clawhammer's got, that's above my pay grade."

"So . . . what's it like out there?" Daddy asks.

Niclaus smiles blandly. "Oh, not too much has changed in the last sixty years. A few more planets colonized. Still no alien intelligence. Earth's as overpopulated and smelly as ever." This is obviously a practiced statement. There's something this man doesn't want to say. How could nothing change in sixty years? Even here on Bella Inizio things have changed.

"What about on the planet?" Daddy asks, as if he doesn't notice that Niclaus is trying to evade his questions. But of course he does notice. Daddy notices things and waits to act.

"Well, nature's busy reclaiming the town." Niclaus waves at the town rising out of the cleared acres behind us, which is much larger than it was when the colonists uploaded. "Trees growing through floors, that kind of thing."

Daddy nods. "Wish we could have stayed. I wanted it to work out, but it just wasn't safe there."

I don't know what comes over me, but I have the sudden urge to say it. A child would say it, I think. A child wouldn't understand why she shouldn't.

"I had a sister who died." I look up at Niclaus with big eyes.

Daddy's face is blank.

"I'm really sorry," Niclaus says. He's responding to me, but he's speaking to Daddy.

"Thank you," Daddy says, voice even. "My wife also died of the gastro."

"Gastro?" Niclaus's gaze goes to the colonists, who are milling about pretending to talk among themselves, taking furtive glances at us.

"You don't know?" Daddy asks.

"About a disease?" Niclaus grips his helmet. "No, and thank Cheezus for this hazmat suit. Told us we could wear them if we wanted to but there was no need. Bella Inizio was rated risk: low." He shakes his head. "Well, I've still got it on." I imagine this man's body someplace dark, the helmet on his head, things stuck to his skull. It gives me the creeps.

"What'd they tell you about why we uploaded?"

Niclaus sighs. "Didn't tell us a thing. Figured being a pioneer's harder than it looks."

"I never would have left if it was just that," Daddy says. He's trying to keep his voice light, but I hear the anger. Daddy wouldn't have given up. Daddy traded the planet for this universe to save us. That's what he thinks.

"I understand. It was a bad turn you had."

"I'm going to build a spaceship," I say, pretending like I've understood nothing. "Daddy says we have lots of planets out there just like you do."

"That's true," Niclaus says. "Not quite so many as

we have, but you've got plenty." He manages to smile at me, but it's forced. "You know, I have a daughter about your age. Her name's Talia. She's really into space too."

"Well, we should make our way to my house," Daddy says. "I've been compiling the reports of anomalies. It's mostly elements gone missing. A few transpositions."

"Okay, okay, that's great," Niclaus says. "Should be an easy fix if that's all it is. One thing about Clawhammer, they don't have too many glitches. Now, Pocket Parts." He whistles. "I'm all over the galaxy reprogramming the laws of physics."

Daddy turns to the crowd and raises his arms. "I know everyone wants to meet the visitor, but first I've got to show him the data. We'll head to my house, and when we're done with that, we'll offer him some hospitality. Don't know how long he's got, but first thing is making sure all our elements are where they're supposed to be!"

"Three hours," Niclaus says. "My buddy's got instructions to pull me out."

"Fine, fine," Daddy says. "Let's not waste any more time then. I'd hate to have you come all this way and miss the culinary delights of Bella Inizio. Especially since you won't gain weight in here, right?"

Niclaus laughs. "Lead the way, then. Let's hurry!"

"Didn't you all hear that?" Daddy shouts. "You've got an hour to cook your asses off!"

The crowd whoops. I catch a glimpse of Briana, and she's smiling too. Kady is jumping up and down. As one, the people turn and head back toward town. They're all in young bodies, and healthy, so they move fast. I wonder how it looks to this man from the real world. He must have seen old people and people who were sick. No wonder he seemed so upset to learn that there was a disease on the real Bella Inizio.

If I escape, will I be susceptible to disease? No, no, I tell myself. If I escape, it will be to another simulated universe. I can't go to the real world. That isn't possible. People from outside go into universes to save themselves. If I escape, my life can only get better. I have to focus on my plan.

8

DADDY AND NICLAUS make small talk as we walk. Daddy tells Niclaus about how we expanded the town and the surrounding farmland and eventually spread out to the Western Settlement. He peppers his explanations with *just like we planned to do out there*, and *I bet on Earth they don't need to*, and other hints that Daddy wants more information about the real world. But Niclaus just nods along and says things like *impressive* and *interesting*.

I wonder if there's a rule that he's not supposed to tell us much. Has something bad happened? Or is Clawhammer worried that we'll ask to be let out again? At this thought, I have to make an effort not to dig my nails into Daddy's hand. I tell myself this guy's trying to be polite, just doing what for him is a routine job.

I imagine having a job, having something to do

other than go to kindergarten, being able to help others instead of being the one who needs help. Being able to live in my own house. I stop the thoughts there, because there's so much, so many freedoms, so many things children can't have.

We walk so quickly that I have to almost run to keep up. Daddy never lets go of my hand, and I don't let go of his until we reach our house.

"I've got an interface in here," Daddy says. "Got reports of the missing elements. Don't know what several species of bird and a pickup truck have in common. Or what they both have in common with a drawer full of socks, if you believe that. I thought each bird would be its own element. We've lost some singletons." We're walking down the hall now toward Daddy's office.

"They're probably interconnected," Niclaus says. "The birds, I mean. Glitch in one affected them all, but that's a pretty easy fix. Don't know why they did it that way, but I can decouple them. Make sure it won't happen again."

"That won't take too much storage?"

"Naw, you guys have plenty for what you've got here. I'll doublecheck the emergent elements though. Make sure there's no glitch in the growth algorithms."

They reach Daddy's office, and he lets go of my hand. "Ella, you can play in your room. We'll be out in a few minutes."

"There's going to be a party?" I ask.

"Yes, a big party." Daddy smiles down at me. He looks like a father smiling at a little girl.

I know I'll never get Niclaus alone at the party. After we leave this house, he'll be pulled in a million directions. He'll exit our universe, fix our glitches, and never be seen again. And my next chance won't come for another sixty years. I've spent a thousand hours thinking about what I'd do in this moment. Now that it's here, I realize how stupid my plan is. It's not a plan really, it's just a hope.

"Sounds like fun," Niclaus says as they disappear into Daddy's office and Daddy closes the door in front of me. I don't go to my room, though. I go to the living room and pace around. I circle and circle and circle, and I know that with every moment I'm acting less like a child. I'm letting my entire façade, and everything I need to survive, fall apart because this moment is too important and too quick, and I have to hang on.

Be the same as you always are, Ella, Samantha says in my imagination.

"You've been Ella all your life," I whisper to myself.

"Ella!" Daddy stands in the hallway holding his hand out. Niclaus is behind him.

"I want to go with the spaceman!" I say. I run up to him, hold out my hand, and look up.

He looks down at me and smiles. "Sure, honey,

that's fine with me." He takes my outstretched hand, and I wonder if he can feel the sweat. I wonder if he can tell my heart is beating. I wonder if he thinks of me as human being, or if he thinks of me as an element. He must *know* I'm as good as human, but does he know in his heart?

"Ella, come with me," Daddy says.

"Really, it's fine," says Niclaus. He leans down to me. "Did you know there's a planet where everything is orange?"

"Orange?" I ask. We're moving toward the door now. Daddy is leading us. He's letting me hold the spaceman's hand.

"The trees, the grass, the birds, even the bugs— all as orange as a carrot." We're out on the street. We're three blocks from the meeting hall. I slow my steps a little bit.

"Why?"

"I don't know for sure, but it's something in the air. When people went there, their skin turned orange too."

Daddy walks fast. He gains ground. He's not far ahead, and what if he turns back? I can't wait any longer.

"Niclaus," I whisper. I lift my head up. I grip his hand. I look directly into his eyes. "I'm fifty-eight years old. He's forcing me to live like a little kid. His dead daughter. Help me."

Niclaus stares down at me. He's frozen.

"Does it hurt to be orange?" I ask in my Ella voice.

"Special access to human elements," Niclaus whispers. *Yes,* I think. *Yes, he understands.* And he said *elements,* but he also said *human.*

"Take me with you."

Niclaus forces a smile, and we keep walking, but he slows his steps a little bit with me. Daddy pulls a tiny bit farther ahead. "No, that's the best part! It doesn't hurt at all. You're just orange all over. Here." He pinches my nose. "And here." He taps one of my ears, and then he whispers. "I don't have the equipment for that."

My vision blurs. I knew he'd say no. I knew it would be impossible. I planned for this. I stumble over my feet, and he holds me up by the hand that still holds mine tightly.

"Delete me."

Daddy is slowing his steps to wait for us. He's too close now. "Really?" Daddy says. "Orange planets?"

"Oh yeah," Niclaus says. "Talk about surprises. It wasn't like that on the survey. Turns out it's only for half the year." Niclaus and Daddy continue talking. Something about the colonists and their orange hair. Something about new planets colonized. Niclaus is telling Daddy things he wouldn't have said before. He's trying to help me. But will he do what I need him to do?

I don't want to die. But I can't live here for another sixty years. I need to find out if there's another way. I need to know if he's telling me no because it's hard or because he truly can't do it. I need to show him how bad it is. If he has a daughter, maybe he sees her in me. Maybe looking like I do will help.

Niclaus taps the back of my hand. One, two, three slow taps. We're approaching the meeting hall. We're approaching a crowd of people outside the doors. They're coming toward us.

I squeeze his hand back. I don't know what we're telling each other, but I want it to mean that he's going to help me, or that he hasn't forgotten me, or something.

"Well, I'm gonna have to give you back to your dad now," Niclaus says, smiling down at me. "I hope we get a chance to say goodbye, but if not, I'll be back after I fix the glitches. I always check in to make sure it's all good." He reaches down and tweaks my nose again, and then he lets go of my hand. He turns toward the people and holds up his hands, laughing. "Hey, hey, I'm here. I heard there was food!"

For a few long seconds, I'm standing alone and unnoticed in the crowd. My eyes find the holes in the crowd of people, the path through them. I'm always doing this: looking for a path, planning a strategy for running, thinking about making a break for it. Always planning, never doing. Always too afraid of what Daddy will do to me or somebody else.

Nobody can help me except the one person who's outside of Daddy's control.

I don't see Daddy until he's already taken my hand again. The crowd makes room for us. Daddy talks to people, laughs, assures everyone that the missing elements will be returned, that nothing bad will happen now, that everything's fine.

People swirl around us. There's so much joy, so much laughter. The meeting hall is filled with the scents of so many foods I can't pick them all out. There's roasted meat and sharp spice and alcohol and sweetness and smoke. People sit at the long tables and eat. Someone puts a plate in front of me: meat steaming with gravy; fresh vegetables that probably came from Briana's farm. I'm the farthest thing from hungry, but I pick up my fork.

Daddy pulls my plate toward him and begins cutting up my meat. He cuts, cuts, cuts, until it's in tiny pieces.

"Here you go, pumpkin," he says. He picks up the knife that was part of my table setting and moves it to the left of his fork. Too dangerous for a little kid, obviously.

I don't say thank you. Nobody expects it from five-year-old. I take a bite, and it's good. Still, my tongue feels like leather. My eyes search for Niclaus, who's at the other end of the table, at the head. He's digging into his plate, stopping to comment on how good it is. I can't hear what he's saying, but from the way the women laugh, I imagine it's something like, *best pot roast in the galaxy*, or *never had anything this good*. He pats his stomach, and I know he's saying something like, *glad I can't gain weight in here*.

He only looks at me once, and it's just for a second, and it's only to give me the kind of smile you'd give a child. *But he knows,* I tell myself. *He knows. He knows.*

A woman offers him wine, and he declines. A man offers him Bella Inizio's best whiskey, and he declines that too. I wonder if he can get drunk in here, or if there's some other reason. I've never had alcohol, but I know I don't like the way it makes people act, the way they get too close to you, and talk too much, and smell. People whisper after he declines the whiskey, but he doesn't seem fazed. He keeps eating and eating.

Camilla brings out a cake, and she talks to Niclaus as she hands him a piece, bending her mouth right down to his ear. Other people bring more cakes. People all over town must have run home and baked like madmen to get all of them ready.

The plates go around, and I end up with a big piece, way too big for an adult, much less a kid. I eat mindlessly, letting the sugar pass over my tongue unnoticed. I wish I could gain weight—a popular obsession with flesh-and-blood people, I gather from all the books I've read. Instead, I'll get a stomach ache. Excess food hurts us just enough so that we don't go overboard, don't enjoy our lives too much.

And then the party is dispersing. People are clearing plates away. Drunk people sway and talk too loudly and press through the doors together into the afternoon sunlight. Niclaus stands, whispers to Camilla, looks at his arm, must be telling her he has to leave.

Daddy goes over to him, and I'm alone again, except for the empty plate where my cake was. Niclaus comes over to me and leans down. Daddy is right behind him.

"Did you like the party?" I ask.

"Best party in the whole world," he says. "Hey, I'll be back tomorrow. Maybe you can show me around?"

"Yeah!" I say.

"Okay, okay. Well, I have to get back now or my buddy will get worried." He tips an imaginary hat at me, and then he's walking away with Daddy. Briana appears at my side.

"Phil asked me to walk you home," Briana says.

"I can't believe how much cake you got!" Kady says to me.

I giggle. "Daddy didn't notice."

"Wonderful. Now I've got two kids on a sugar high," Briana says. "Don't let her fool you, Ella. She got a huge piece herself." We begin walking, working our way through the dispersing crowd until we're in the relatively empty street.

"Do you think he'll bring the birds back?" Kady asks.

I'm surprised she understands that the birds were part of a glitch, but maybe I shouldn't be. One thing I've learned in all these years of being five years old is that five-year-olds are smarter than adults think they are.

"Yeah, I heard him say it," I tell her.

"Well, that's a relief," Briana says. "I saw you walking with him."

I look up at her. "He listened to me."

Briana blinks and quickly wipes a tear out of her eye. I'm not sure what she's crying for: for me, or for herself, or because someone might help me, or because she knows what I'll try to do if he can't. Or maybe she's just crying because sometimes people do that.

We get to Daddy's house, and we all go inside to wait until Daddy comes back to watch over me. Kady decides we should play hide-and-seek, and so that's what we do. I hide in one of the kitchen cabinets while Briana walks around calling my name, pretending she doesn't know where I am. Her voice is light, but I hear the cracks. I know she'll find me, and I know I'll have to make it through the rest of the day.

But tomorrow, something will happen. Never in my whole life have I been more sure of that.

9

I WAKE UP to a strange sound. I lie in bed listening for a long time, trying to figure out what I'm hearing. When I finally understand, I sit up and pull my blankets around me.

Birds. So many birds. Chirping away outside my window like they used to do years ago. They disappeared slowly, one species or one bird at a time, maybe. I can't place the moment I realized they were gone. But I have a feeling that even if I live a long time, I won't forget the moment they came back.

I listen and listen, making sure it's true.

If Niclaus could replace the birds, then he's real. He can go outside our universe and fix it—fix us, fix me. He knows how to do it, I feel sure. He can. With the right equipment? Or without it. Why would he tell me he was coming back, give me hope, unless there was some chance of saving me?

I race from my bedroom. "Daddy, birds!"

He's sitting at the kitchen table, a steaming mug of coffee next to him. He smiles, and I smile back. I smile because this might be the last day. Because once I'm gone, I'll never have to see his smile again. And because there are birds where there were no birds before, because like Samantha said, anything is possible.

Are you possible? I ask her.

She doesn't answer while Daddy makes me porridge. She doesn't answer while I eat and while I put on my good pants and my favorite shirt with three bright red hearts on it, or while we leave the house and climb into Daddy's car. But she doesn't say no.

"I thought you might like to see him appear," Daddy says.

"Now?" My voice squeaks; I try too hard to sound like Ella.

"After we collect some reports." Daddy drives around town and stops at what seems like every house. At the meeting house, he gets on the radio and talks to someone in the Western Settlement. I think about asking to talk to Samantha, just to make him pretend she's there, but instead, I act like a bored five-year-old. I wriggle around in the passenger seat, asking when he's going to be done and when we can go see the spaceman.

Daddy smiles indulgently and tells me *soon*.

It feels like hours later, but finally Daddy gets back into the car. "Sounds like that's everything," he says. He pats my knee. "This world is a pretty great place."

"Did that lady get her socks back?" I wriggle in my seat and peer out the window.

"Yep. Even the one that had no match." He chuckles. "We said we wanted things to be realistic, but maybe we should have said socks have to stay together."

I pretend like I don't understand what he's talking about. There are lots of things I'd make not realistic if I was in charge. Pain. Frosts like the one we had three years ago that destroyed all of Briana's vegetables. People being in charge of other people. But there are other things I'd make more realistic. Me. Earth being out there somewhere filled with people. People not disappearing because someone flicked his fingers into an interface.

I guess realistic is whatever you want the world to be.

We drive on the road through the woods past Day One Meadow and stop on the far side. There's nothing here except the back edge of the meadow, filled with long grasses. And birdsong. Loud, almost viciously joyful birdsong. Part of me hates it, their joy. These birds are free. Maybe they're brand-new birds who haven't experienced pain yet. Maybe Niclaus pulled them back from somewhere that . . .

don't think about it . . . don't hope . . . some place where deleted elements go. But they have something I don't, and I want to cry, but I have to smile. For one more hour, for one more day—I don't know. Mentally, I grit my teeth.

I smile big. "Where is he?"

"Any minute now, pumpkin. Wait for it!" We stand together, and the birds sing, and the clouds float by in the blue sky, and then suddenly, he appears a few feet in front of us.

One second, nothing. Then: Niclaus wearing his spacesuit and his helmet.

He reaches to his neck and does something with his fingers, and then he removes the helmet from his head, and he's standing there with his hair rumpled and a smile on his face.

"Welcome!" Daddy approaches him and relates the news that all of our missing elements appear to be fixed. "How long do you have this morning?"

"Well, we're scheduled for liftoff in three hours, presuming we're all done here. Clawhammer pays well, but not a lot of down time, you know?"

"Sure, I remember how it is," Daddy says. "One reason we decided to try colonization. So many of us were tired of the old grind."

"I hear you. But you know, I promised little Ella I'd let her show me around. You want to take a walk?" He grins at me. "You got a favorite place to fish?" As he says the words, I become aware of the sound of the river in the background. With all the birds, I hadn't even noticed it. But it's genius. Even if Daddy's near, we might be able to talk.

"Daddy and I catch ones like this"—I move my hands wide apart—"and they have huge noses." I put my hand to my face, fingers out. These fish have crazy faces, soft parts splayed out, always moving as if grasping for something.

"That's not too far away," Daddy says, and he waves an arm and begins walking.

I grab Niclaus's hand, and we all walk for a while without talking. Niclaus looks around him as if he's taking it all in. He has a little smile on his face as if the birds mean something to him too. But I can't presume to read the mind of a man from Earth, who's living in what to us is basically the far future.

We reach the river, and I drag him down to the bank, where he holds my hand tightly and crouches down. Daddy sits on a rock watching the river and us, but Niclaus's plan has worked perfectly. At least, if it hasn't and Daddy can hear us, we'll find out.

"Ella, I don't have anything on my ship that can transfer your program. It's a special type of storage unit. Very dangerous to try any other way. You'd be dissipated or corrupted."

"I don't care," I whisper, smiling my face off. "Try anything."

"I won't risk your life," he says. He looks right into my eyes, and I think I see that he understands, that he knows what he's condemning me to.

"Then delete me," I whisper. "Daddy caught one bigger than that."

"Wow, that's impressive. We will never harm a human under our care." He says it like he's reciting something, like he's reading it straight out of a book.

"I . . ." My mind races on all the ways I could beg. He's implied that there's some way to help me, but it's risky. I'm willing to take any risk. I don't care if there's a one-percent chance of me surviving.

"But at the next tune-up, I'll see if I can do anything."

"Sixty years from now?" I can't keep myself smiling. That's a whole lifetime. That's too long. I can't take sixty more days of this.

"It won't be me, but I can pass on a message. I promise I will, Ella." He squeezes my hand.

"You . . . a message."

"What say we take a walk down to the fork?" Daddy says. He leads the way, and I follow with the spaceman. We walk there, we look at fish, Daddy and Niclaus talk about the flora and fauna, and then we walk back. Every step through the woods is torture. Every second of the next sixty years will be torture. All so that I can hope that Niclaus, who'll be old and off somewhere retired, uploaded, or dead, can pass on a message, and that someone will act on it. I can't. I can't. I can't.

I wait for something from Samantha. A *you can*. But she's silent. There's no *you can*. Not for sixty more years.

And then we're back at the edge of Day One Meadow, and Niclaus lets go of my hand.

"Thank you for welcoming me to Bella Inizio," he says to Daddy. And then to me: "You're a great kid." I see a flash in his eyes of something sad, something sorry, and then he's gone.

10

THIS SITUATION is what I've been watching for, why I've spent all that time lying still on the ground on our attic floor. I don't know if I ever admitted it to myself. I definitely didn't think it out in a coherent sentence in my head. But I was learning how Daddy entered the system and how he found a person and what he did.

Daddy drops me by Camilla Wolkowitz's kindergarten class.

"Really sorry to bring her late, but I wanted to give her a special treat. Because she's been such a good kid lately." He ruffles my hair.

"No problem, Phil," Camilla says at the door to her classroom. She smiles blandly.

"Have a good time at the party yesterday?" Daddy asks.

"Yeah, it was a lot of fun. Did you get any news from outside?"

Daddy whistles. "Well, not as much as I wanted. Tell you about it sometime soon."

"Okay, sounds good." Camilla puts a hand to my back and ushers me in to the classroom.

I sit in the back and pretend to listen.

When Daddy arrives to pick me up, I leave with him. I think about saying goodbye to Camilla. It would be the polite thing after everything she did for me. Instead, I leave without saying a word. I sit through the dinner Daddy cooks. I listen to Daddy on the walkie-talkie, telling someone about what Niclaus said about the outside world: about the colony that turned orange, about the cluster of inhabitable planets on the far side of the galaxy that's becoming the new center of human civilization.

"So unlikely to find so many planets close together," Daddy says.

And I don't care. I don't care. I don't care.

I change into my pajamas. I brush my teeth. I climb under the covers and listen as Daddy reads me a bedtime story. It's an old Earth story about a girl and a dog, and I know it by heart, and I mouth the words without really hearing them. I close my eyes as Daddy turns the light off, and I wait. The seconds and minutes and hours go past, and then I climb out of bed and walk to Daddy's office.

The door is locked now, but I know where the key is. I get it from its hiding place in the back of a high cupboard. I climb like a champion, and I don't make noise. I unlock the door. I walk inside and close it behind me. There's a lamp on the desk that shouldn't show too much under the door, and I turn it on to the dimmest setting. I'm standing now where Vera was lying that first time and many times after that.

The last time I was in this room and not just watching from above was forty-seven years ago. I was eleven. It was the middle of the day, but it was Rest Day, and we were all in the house: me, Daddy, Samantha. I had been playing in the back yard, using a large stick as a bat, chasing an unripe piece of fruit around the yard like it was a ball. From all the way out there, I heard Daddy shouting. I couldn't understand what he was saying, but one word came through loud and clear: *interfere*. And then, *Ella*.

I ran back into the house and around the corner into the hall. My heart was beating through my chest, and I didn't know what to do. Now I could hear them clearly.

"Phil, it's not right. She's such a smart kid. She deserves to be able to learn and grow."

"I don't want to hear any more, Sam."

"But you have to. This can't go on any longer.

What are you going to do when she's fifty years old? A hundred? Are you going to keep making her act like she's a little kid?" There was a crashing sound, and Samantha squealed in pain.

I ran into the doorway and stopped cold. Samantha was sitting on the ground, leaning on her hands as if she'd just caught herself. Daddy towered over her. His face was lit by the green glow of the interface.

"You will not change my perfect daughter," Daddy said. He turned and began flipping through the screens.

"Phil." Samantha stood up. She paused for a few seconds, her breathing heavy. "Phil, I love Ella, more than anything in the world. I feel like she's my own daughter. All I want is what's best for her."

Daddy turned to her. "You see this?" he said, pointing to a string of numbers. "That's your code. That's what you are. All I have to do is—" A few inches from the interface, he swiped two fingers.

"Phil, what the fuck?" Samantha said. "You're going to kill me? What's my sin? Trying to talk some sense into you?"

Daddy moved his fingers closer. I was right in his line of sight, but he didn't see me. All he saw was Samantha.

"Phil, Jesus. Don't . . ." Her voice rose in pitch. She held her hands up. "I'm not saying anything, okay? We both love Ella. We both just want what's best for her."

"Do you promise never to mention this again?" Daddy held the fingers still.

"I . . . it's not right, Phil. You know that."

Daddy swiped his fingers across the interface.

Samantha screamed. She fell to her knees, and she put her hands on her head, and it took a long time. Maybe it was a minute, or half a minute, or a few seconds, but it felt like it took a million years. I was frozen in place, my voice choked in my throat. I had seen Daddy delete other people, but the person had never been in the room with him. I'd never seen how much it hurt.

Samantha's voice cut off as if someone had pressed a *stop* button. She was gone.

Daddy looked down at where she had been.

"Oh Jesus," he said. He turned to the interface. He flipped through screens. "Where is she?" he said to himself. "Where is she? Sam, I didn't mean it. I wasn't thinking." He stood there at that interface for hours, and then for days and weeks afterward, but he was never able to bring her back. He was never able to undo what he'd done to the woman he was supposed to love. And once I'm gone, he won't be able to bring me back either.

Now, I'm standing where Samantha was standing as she begged Daddy not to delete her. This is the spot where bad things happen.

I've never actually used what I've learned. Maybe it won't work. Deep inside me, something stirs. A part of me that wants this not to work. But I take a deep breath and stuff it down. I turn on the computer, and it lights up. The interface appears in the air. I input Daddy's code. I'm standing so close to the symbols that I'm almost inside them. It takes me a minute to orient myself to being down here instead of up in the attic watching. But I see everything with perfect clarity. I've been waiting for this moment for most of my life.

I know how to find myself, and I do.

The overhead light switches on.

"Ella, what are you doing?" Daddy stands in the doorway. He's wearing pajama pants and nothing on top. There's hair growing in a t-shape on his chest. Probably it was once gray, but now it's not. He points a finger at me, smooth and ageless.

"I think you know," I tell him. I look up at him, but I'm not a child looking up at a father anymore. I look at him with my own eyes.

He holds up both hands. "Ella, step back from the interface." I see him calculating the distance between us, wondering if he can stop me. He can see the symbols as clearly as I can, how easy it would be for me to swipe myself out of existence.

"You're the reason I'm doing this," I say, holding

his eyes. "I'm not Ella. I'm not five years old. You've tortured me for fifty-eight years, and I won't do it anymore."

"Ella, stop this. You don't know what you're doing. It's dangerous." He's using the Daddy voice. He's still talking down to me.

"Maybe you can make another Ella. Maybe you will. But you can't make another *me*. You can't bring me back. I saw you try to save Samantha. After you killed her. I saw you, and you couldn't do it."

"Please don't do this," Daddy says.

"What else am I supposed to do!" I yell. My hand is in the air, in the exact spot.

"I love you so much," Daddy says. "When you died, I wanted to die too. You were everything to me. I created this whole universe to bring you back."

"She would have grown up!" The tears are escaping from my eyes, and from his. The room swims, but my hand is steady. I know how to do it. I'm not losing my chance.

"But you don't have to."

"You created me to hurt me. All you've ever done is hurt me."

"You never have to know what it's like to have a child, to lose them, to see a wife die, to see anyone die. You can live forever protected and safe and loved." Daddy takes a step forward.

"I hope you live forever knowing I hate you, and

Ella would hate you. You're a monster, and no one will ever love you again." I swipe my fingers at just the right place.

It hurts, and now I know why Samantha screamed. Now I know that most pain in this world must be muted, that I've never felt anything like this, and I never could. Daddy runs toward me and grabs at me with both arms, but his arms go through me. He falls to the ground on hands and knees, and he screams as if it's him dying, as if he's feeling this same pain, and maybe he is, and I'm glad, and I let the pain run through me and rip me apart from the inside out.

11

I SCREAM before I feel the pain. I'm on the ground on hands and knees. I try to grab with my fingers, but there's something hard beneath them. My knees press into the hard surface too. My entire body is aflame, and my voice escapes from my mouth loud and feral. I scream until my throat hurts, and my voice suddenly stops, and the pain is coursing through my flesh, and I can't see anything. And then it begins to subside, and I gasp for breath, and I calm myself and try to think, and I remember what I just did.

And it must not have worked. I must still be alive.

I press my hands into the floor, and it's cold beneath me. It's not the floor of Daddy's office, which had a rug. Am I in the attic? Did he shut me up there?

"Ella." Someone says the word. Something touches my hand. I blink, and I look down at it, and I see that on top of my hand is a reddish glove. Another hand, touching mine. "Ella, don't be afraid. You're all right."

I slide my hand away and push myself up. I hear the humming the same second as I see his face. Behind the clear face shield of the spacesuit helmet is a face I know. Niclaus. The humming is everywhere, all around me. I stare at his face, see him crouching on his knees in front of me. He's wearing the same suit, but it's dirty. Brown streaks float up his arms. The orange color of the front of the suit is faded. This suit has been lived in. Sweat drips down Niclaus's face. Blotches mar his pale skin. His hair is matted where the nodes that now barely recede from his head must have been stuck.

"Spaceman," I whisper.

"You've royally screwed things up for me," Niclaus says.

"What the fuck is—" Another man's voice cuts through the humming. "Oh for the love of Christ. Are you fucking kidding me?" He strides through what I realize must be machines. Some are large and some are smaller, all metal. That's where the humming's coming from. I pull a word from the back of my brain, something I've read about but never seen. *Servers.* The man is taller than Niclaus. Behind his spacesuit helmet, his face is covered with a thick beard. I can't see his eyes behind the glare of some light coming from above, reflecting off the face shield.

"Give us a minute," Niclaus says.

"Give you a minute?" The man comes closer and stands with both gloved hands on his hips. "There's not enough time in our lives to unfuck this shit."

Niclaus turns on him. "What was I supposed to do? She was trying to delete herself. If I hadn't been taking one last look at the system—"

"Then she'd be deleted," the man says. "Better than having to explain this."

Niclaus presses a hand to his face mask as if he wants to wipe his face, and then angrily moves his hand away. "I know we can't explain it, okay? We'll think of something."

"Hmm, okay. A little girl managed to survive alone for sixty years on this godforsaken planet, without ever aging a day, and without encountering any of the fabricators or drillers, or anything that has eyes on it."

"Maybe she didn't come from here."

"So instead of going to our next assignment we redirected the AI to take us to some other planet, and while there we kidnapped a little girl! That's a much better explanation!"

"She stowed away," Niclaus says.

"Man, that's not possible. You fucking know that."

"Well, neither is the truth, Erickson. Neither is the freaking truth."

The two men stare at each other. Niclaus folds his arms across his chest. Erickson throws his arms up. "She's your problem. You can't come up with something better, I go straight to the Academy. I tell them what you did, and you deal with it." Erickson turns and stomps his way back through the machines. I follow him with my eyes until he reaches a door that opens to. . . .

"Where am I?" I ask.

Niclaus turns back to me. "You're on Bella Inizio."

"There's another Bella Inizio simulation?" My eyes are locked on that open door. I could swear I hear birds through the humming of the machines. But maybe it's my imagination.

"This is the *real* Bella Inizio," Niclaus says.

I stare at him.

Niclaus holds out a hand and helps me up. The pain has subsided to a dull ache. It takes a long minute before he continues. "As far as every human in existence is concerned, this is the real world, the real universe. But it's also a simulation." He turns his head and tries to touch his face again. "Nobody knows this, and nobody can know, do you understand?"

"No." And yes. And my heart is swelling, and adrenaline is pumping through my body, and I want to scream again with joy. Because I'm in the real world, the world with Earth, and I'm not in Daddy's world, and I don't care if it's a simulation or not, because it's a different universe, and Daddy's locked away and can't find me, and I'm free.

"Here's the short version. For most of history, no one knew this was a simulation. We thought this was the real, physical world. Yeah, people speculated, but there was no way to prove anything. Then, about eighty years ago, Clawhammer and its partners developed faster-than-light travel. They began building spaceships that supposedly use an artificial intelligence to fold space, thereby allowing a ship to pass almost instantly from one region of space to another." Niclaus looks at me expectantly.

"I may not really be five years old, but I don't know a lot about space travel," I say.

"Well, it violated the laws of physics. It wasn't possible."

"I'm sorry, I still don't understand." Maybe in this new world, I am like a five-year-old. I haven't had a real education even in the context of Bella Inizio.

"Neither did almost anyone else, so don't feel bad. The corporations came up with this great explanation. They had math; they had mumbo-jumbo. They convinced the physicists. And why not, since the technology worked? But this was about the same time as Clawhammer and Pocket Parts and a couple other companies started building robust simulated universes. They endowed a Technicians Academy to train people to take care of them. And we learned how to change the laws of physics within these universes. There were a few people at the top of the Academy who realized, hey, the fact that something that should be impossible is possible means something fishy's going on."

Niclaus tries to rub his face again. "Cheezus, I'm sick of this darn helmet. Anyway, they decided there was a way to test it. What if they could figure out a way to remove an element from a simulation created by Clawhammer and plunk it into the real world, just like you move an element from one simulated universe to another? If that was possible, it would prove that our universe is a simulation too."

"Me," I say.

"Right. I mean, they started with simpler elements, like your missing socks. But they figured out a way to level something up. The first time they succeeded, it was a table. A little one like people keep next to their beds. It was real. It was solid. It was just like any other table. Poof, matter from nothing. Impossible."

My mind races. I know what this means. And I can tell Niclaus doesn't want to me to say it. "Then we can move everyone," I say. "We can take the colonists out again, save them from Daddy. Camilla and Briana and Kady and everyone, all the people Daddy's hurting."

"No problem at all," Erickson says from behind Niclaus, sarcasm dripping from his voice. "Couldn't have anticipated that request. Listen, we gotta go. We have five appointments on Earth this week. We're looking at like four hours of sleep tonight as it is."

"Okay." Niclaus reaches down like he's about to take my hand, then rethinks it. "Sorry, that's a habit. I know you're not a kid, I promise."

"Can you fix me? Make me grow?"

Niclaus hesitates, and I know what he's going to say. I want to fall back to the ground and scream.

"I leveled you up as an intact element," he says. "For all of us, the elements of this universe, our parameters are controlled somewhere else. As far as we know, there's no way to change an element in our universe from inside it." He's lying, or he's not telling the whole truth. I can feel it. I can see it in his eyes, the way he doesn't quite look at me. My mind starts working, but I don't grasp the answer. It's there though, somewhere close.

"If you start in with that God shit, I'm going to leave you both behind," Erickson says. "I'm doing one last external sweep. Be on board in one hour or I swear to the Programmer-In-The-Sky, I'm leaving you here on this wrecked piece of shit."

"He means it," Niclaus says. "We can't move anyone else. Not only would it be a colossal breach of contract, but you're hard enough to explain. And keep quiet. No one can know where you came from."

"Why not?" I try to keep my voice calm, but it cracks. I've spent my whole life keeping calm and quiet.

"It'll be faster if you wait outside while I close up in here. Gotta make sure it's all good for the next sixty years. Short answer: lots of bad stuff will happen. I'll give you a longer answer in a minute."

"Okay," I say. Because I can see that this isn't the time to push. I can see that he wasn't supposed to save me and there's a part of him that wishes he didn't. And he's not going to do anything else for me right now. "I'll wait outside."

I slip past Niclaus the spaceman and walk through the machines. They're taller than me, and I want to stop and look at them. I want to examine every inch and understand how these metal things and the cables connecting them make a universe, how real live people can be inside. I want to just stop and contemplate it, to try to understand what it means that I was in there and now I'm not, and now maybe I'm somewhere else, in another server. But Niclaus told me to go, and I know when to do what people say.

I did what Daddy said because if I didn't he'd hurt somebody, and I did what Briana said or what Camilla said because they were good people who wanted to help me, at least for a while. And I have to believe that Niclaus is one of those people. I've believed that since before I even knew his name was Niclaus, since I first learned there was such thing as a Technician. Because sometimes you just have to believe things. Sometimes you have to hope. Or. . . .

I step through the open door and into the meadow. It takes me a second to realize what I'm looking at. The day is sunny. There are fluffy clouds in the sky. There's grass beneath my feet, but it's not tall like it was before. It's short and sparse.

I drop to my knees.

Or . . . you die.

I was going to die, I realize. I gasp for breath. The air is sharp, different than I'm used to. There's something bad about it, but it's air in my lungs. I'm not dead, but I came so close. I'm shaking, and I wipe sweat from my face, because it's hot here—too hot. And I look out toward where the road should be, toward where the forest should be, and there's no forest. I shouldn't be able to see the city from here because of all the trees, but I can. I can see something that remains of it, but even from this distance I can tell it's all wrong. It's ruined.

The ground in front of me is destroyed—dug up, I realize, probably by mining equipment. And I don't hear birds. I hear silence except for the remnants of the humming behind me.

I didn't want to die. I wanted to live. I wanted to grow. I cry, and I don't know if it's out of relief or because Niclaus just told me I can't grow, or because there are no birds, or because the city is ruined. Because I can't go home, and all I wanted was to be home, to be myself and not Ella, to live there. I didn't want to leave, really. I just wanted freedom.

And now I'm out. And I will never see Daddy again. I'll also never see Kady or Briana or Camilla or any of the other kids or the adults who come to our house to work with Daddy, or anyone. I'll never see anyone I know ever again.

12

THERE'S THE SOUND of a door closing, and a click of finality, and I look up and wipe my eyes on my sleeve, and I see that the building behind me is cylindrical and made of metal, and I can't see where the door was, except Niclaus is standing in front of where it must have been. That's my universe—all it is, all it will ever be.

"Can you bring back a person who was deleted?" I ask Niclaus. "You did it with me."

"You weren't deleted yet," Niclaus says. "I caught you in time."

"But can you?"

"We have to go, Ella." He reaches a hand down to me, and I take it.

"That means you can."

"It means I can't, and we have to go."

I let go of his hand, but I let him lead the way

across what used to be Day One Meadow. It's all broken up now, as if the ground was cut apart and then replaced, and there are grasses growing, but not a lot, and the air smells, and I think about what Daddy would think if he saw this, how he'd hate to see the planet ravaged. Because he loves Bella Inizio, whatever form it takes.

It hits me as I walk across this mined-away former meadow: Daddy could have moved to a universe that was anything, that had any rules. He chose this place, the planet where he lived with Ella and Vera and planned to make a home for himself. And Niclaus lied to Daddy. He didn't tell him the planet was like this. He wanted to make Daddy think Bella Inizio was still his beautiful beginning. That was a kindness by Niclaus but also a dodge.

"Did Clawhammer tell Daddy that the mining wouldn't destroy everything?"

"I don't know what they told him, but the contract doesn't have many conditions. It seems like a waste of an inhabitable planet, doesn't it? But there are so many out there now that we have space-folding travel. Planets we can live on are endless."

"And so are simulated universes," I say.

"Yes."

"How do people choose where to live?" I look up into the sky, and I can't imagine having a choice. I can't truly think about choosing anything for myself.

My universe was one house and one bedroom and one man's decisions. Now, what is it? I still look five years old, and the thought twists my stomach into a knot.

Niclaus laughs. "I don't know if people choose. Sometimes I feel like we're all just being dragged along."

"By a programmer?"

"Don't let Erickson hear you say that. No, I don't think our lives are programmed or predetermined. That's not how the simulations we create work. I just think it's human nature to go where the wind takes us. I became a Technician because a recruiter came to my college. I didn't know he was there. I just walked by the room where he was sitting, spinning a stylus, waiting for some kid to wander in. If I hadn't walked down that hallway, maybe I'd be in medical devices. Or oceanic restoration. Or food service."

"You wouldn't be living on one of those planets?"

"No way. What happened to Phil Harkin happens all the time. It's hard out there. Shorter lives, disease, starvation. Retreating into simulations, usually back on Earth. That building back there? Clawhammer has a whole continent's worth of them."

That brings up so many questions that my mind swirls on them, and then I look up, and I don't know how I missed it before, but across the meadow is a spaceship. I've never seen a spaceship before, but what else could it be? Its design immediately strikes me as tremendously impractical: It's big and metallic and shaped like a bird, with large wings and four spindly legs, and where the bird's spine should be, several cylinders shoot up. It has windows, but from here they're black. We trudge toward it, and as we come closer, I see that there's a patch of green, a place where the grass is still growing, where the ground hasn't been destroyed.

"What's that?" I ask.

"I don't know if you want to see that."

"Don't hide things from me," I say. "Please. I won't tell anyone where I came from. Just tell me the truth about things."

"Well, I'll show you then." We walk, and I hurry, because I'm drawn to the green, to this patch of life. As we get closer, I see there are slabs of rock standing in rows.

"What is this?" I walk toward the nearest rock, and Niclaus stands back. There are words on it. I read out loud: "Cassandra Chen-Belize. It's just a name." There's another stone close by, and I read that name too. "Caliman Chen-Belize. And then, Zaria Chen-Belize." I stare at the names, knowing I should understand. I walk down the rows reading the names. One row, two rows, three rows. There are more rows stretching out into a meadow that goes farther than I saw at first. There's a long strip un-touched by mining.

"That was in the contract," Niclaus tells me. "That they'd keep the graveyard intact."

"What's a. . . ." Realization hits me. "These are the people who died of the gastro."

"You've never seen a graveyard before. I'm sorry, I didn't think."

"We don't die." I look up at him. "How can people die here, if this universe is just like ours?"

He shakes his head. "This universe is nothing like yours. It's bigger. It's more like. . . . No one really knows for sure, but I believe this universe is more like the physical one, wherever that is. I believe they created us in their image. So yes, we die. But I also believe that when we die, we emerge a level up, much like what just happened to you."

"Daddy killed people, and they didn't show up here," I say. I look up at him, hope surging through me. "Did they?"

"By killed you mean deleted?"

"Yes," I say. "As punishment. And you can save them, can't you?"

Niclaus shakes his head. "I can't, Ella. I can't." We walk along the rows of graves, and I clench my fists and try not to scream. Because he said he can change the laws of physics. He can do anything. He saved me. *He can.*

Finally, he speaks again. "Phil Harkin's contract with Clawhammer provides that he has control over the creation of human elements. That set of parameters includes deletions, but. . . ." He shakes his head. "It has to include deletion, because if there's an error. . . ." He presses a gloved hand to his faceplate. "I can't break the contract. I broke it by removing you. I'll lose my career. They'll put me in—"

"No, you didn't," I say. "I tried to delete myself. Daddy didn't want me deleted. You probably fulfilled your contract by saving me."

Niclaus stares down at me. "Huh. Maybe."

"But Daddy did delete other people, and you can save them."

"No, Ella." He turns away from me and tries to wipe his face again. I'm glad he's sweating, because he has the power to help, and he won't. But how can I convince him? How can I push without pushing him to leave me here? And then I see them.

"Oh my god." I'm standing in front of a row of three graves. They're taller than the others. It's subtle, but it's real: maybe an inch or two. Vera Harkin. And next to it, Ella Harkin. Philip Harkin. My sister's grave. My mother's grave. "Philip Harkin?" I ask. I take a step back from them and knock into the row behind. My own name on the stone doesn't make me feel the way this does. Because I knew Ella was dead. Somewhere in the back of my mind, I was prepared for that.

"The contract required Clawhammer to bury the bodies. The colonists cut the stones and dug the graves."

"Their own graves."

"They didn't need their bodies anymore, Ella. They have new, better bodies now."

"But you could take them out, and then they'd have bodies again."

"I can't do that."

"You won't."

"Yes." His voice is flat.

"But they're dead. Really. They died and their bodies are buried here. Rotting away, right?"

"You aren't your body. You are an amalgam of quantum states that make up your brain function. All of that was copied perfectly into the people you knew. All of us are just information. Bodies—well, we need them until we don't anymore."

"I don't want to look at this."

"It's time to go anyway," Niclaus says. "Erickson wasn't kidding when he said he'd leave us. We don't want to have to live off of emergency kits until Clawhammer next sends a ship with life support."

I lead the way this time. I walk away from the graveyard, toward the spaceship. Beyond it, where there should be more forest, is dug-up ground. At the edge of the long stretch of wrecked dirt, I see machinery. They're bigger than the fabricators we used to build our colony. I don't see another patch of green in the entire landscape. There's the grave-yard, and then there's nothing. By the time I reach the spaceship, I'm sweating buckets. I don't mean to do it, but I can't stop myself. I turn back and look toward the city.

It's a pile of rubble. Niclaus said there were trees growing through houses, but there aren't. There's not a single green thing in sight.

"That's not your home," Niclaus says. "Remember your home the way I saw it: vibrant, full of life and good food and joy." He puts a gloved hand on my shoulder and pulls me closer.

I wipe the tears from my eyes with my sleeve. All these years I've dreamed of getting away from Daddy, I never realized I'd be sad to leave Bella Inizio. I never thought of it as home because there was never any other place to be. All I wanted was to get away, but I never understood what that meant. I never imagined I would see this, or feel like this ruined planet was something I've lost. But my heart hurts as if someone is squeezing it. This is a terrible thing to happen to my home, and I feel that this is real, and this is what has happened to the place I loved even though I was trapped there.

This is too soon. I've barely come here and now

I'm being rushed away. Alone, without Samantha, without anyone. But I can't stay here in a place this dead. This is my only chance to escape.

"Are you ready?" Niclaus asks gently.

"Yes," I say, wiping a last tear away.

"Okay, the airlock is this way." He turns me around, and we're facing what looks like a blank panel at the bottom of the spaceship, which rises far above our heads. As he finishes speaking, edges appear, and a door slides open, and we're looking at a small, windowless room. I'm standing in front of Niclaus, so I go first. I step off of Bella Inizio and into the belly of the spaceship.

13

WE STAND in the windowless room while air blows on us from all sides. There's a smell too, and a mist in the air, and more blowing, and then a door opens, and we exit into a corridor.

"What was that about?" I ask as Niclaus leads the way. It seems like a maze to me, with several turns and low light and the barest images of doorframes.

"That room cleans us up so we don't bring anything in from outside. It also checks your health to make sure there are no pathogens." He's carrying his helmet now, and sweat pours down his face, plastering his hair to his head. "If we'd had whatever killed your colonists, it most likely would have caught it. The door wouldn't have opened to let us in."

"And then what?"

Niclaus shrugs. "They'd send a transport for us in a case like that. There's a whole fleet of quarantine ships. Cost of doing business. Of course, I might be dead by the time it gets here."

"Can I get sick now?" I ask. Niclaus is leading us into a circular room, where Erickson sits in front of a console. There's a large screen above him, showing rows of symbols. No one answers me.

"Glad you made it," Erickson says, smiling at me. "Might want to strap in." Without the helmet, I can see his eyes. They're large and a soft brown, and they sort of light up his face above his beard. His hair is plastered to his head too, although it's much cooler inside the ship than it was on the planet. "Space-folding doesn't work in the atmosphere. We've got to lift off."

Niclaus takes a seat next to Erickson and helps me strap into a third seat. There are several more seats in a row in front of the console, but no one else seems to be there.

"Okay, kids. Three, two, one." My stomach lurches as I'm thrust into the seat. I barely manage to lean forward before I throw up all over the floor under the console.

Erickson laughs out loud. "I guess there's one way you can get sick. But the other way, probably not. You were programmed to be completely free of disease."

I wipe my mouth. The stink of my throw-up reaches my nose. My stomach is still churning, but my mind is churning faster. "But that means. . . ." I look up at Niclaus, and my mouth drops open. I have to consciously shut it. I think I understand what I was missing before. It all clicks together. "That means that you could upload yourself into a simulation, and then take yourself out again like you just did to me, and you could be free of disease and aging, just like me. You could do that right now and never have to worry about catching anything ever again."

"Smart kid," Erickson says, eying Niclaus.

"So why don't you?"

"Kid, what do you think would happen if we started doing that and people found out about it?"

"Other people would do it?"

"You know what else we can do within the simulations we program? Well, *we* don't program—we troubleshoot, mostly. But Technicians program universes where, say, people fight wars with weapons that can destroy planets, only to 'die' and be reborn again. Because some people want to live in a fucking war game. Some people want to live in universes where dogs can fly and the rivers run chocolate. Whatever we can imagine, we can program."

"And if those weapons came out. . . ."

"Or real people had only chocolate to drink?"

"It would be chaos," Niclaus says. "Pure chaos. Because this universe is a simulation of the real world."

"You believe," Erickson says, rolling his eyes.

"*And*," Niclaus says, rolling his eyes too, "we can't change the elements that are already here."

"Unless you first transfer them to a lower-level universe," I say.

This time, Erickson laughs so hard that he gasps for breath.

Niclaus glares at him. "We don't have enough manpower to transfer every element. There'd be no way to do it before the entire universe became a horror show. And we shouldn't, Ella. We just shouldn't. We have all this." Niclaus pushes a button on the console, and the symbols on the viewscreen disappear, replaced by a view of a field of stars. Below us, Bella Inizio shines. Even with the settlement ruined, there are oceans. There's still some greenery, standing out among the blue and black.

The three of us are silent for a minute as we all take in the view. Even Erickson seems to be giving the universe its due reverence. I forget everything as I look down at the planet. I wasn't pretending when I told Niclaus I was interested in space. I always wanted to be able to see this view, to get to the point in our evolution when we'd explore our universe, such as it was. I thought as a child I'd never be able to. I wonder what *my* Bella Inizio looks like from here, and I have a sudden longing to see it, to know what *my* universe looks like.

"If people found out what was possible, they'd ruin the entire universe," Niclaus says. "That's why no one can know where you came from. That's why I wasn't supposed to save you."

"We're only authorized to save ourselves," Erickson says. "To pull out a Technician who accidentally uploads during a job. It happens sometimes if they stay too long or something glitches. And your savior here refused to learn the code at first. Had to be ordered by the Chancellor herself to be prepared, to never be in a position to leave a fellow Technician behind."

"I knew someday something would happen," Niclaus says. "One of us, somewhere, would crack. I just never thought it would be me. Or maybe I did, and that's why I refused to learn."

"You think the Chancellor looks that good because she uses fancy skin cream?" Erickson pushes some buttons and checks a readout on his console. "Engaging the AI."

Niclaus doesn't say anything. He chews his lip and stares at the starscape. Suddenly, it changes. The entire view turns black. Then without warning: a different starscape. A planet in the distance. A ball of blue and white. I grip my seat handles and blink at the sudden change, but the two of them act like nothing happened.

"It's a wonder we're not all walking ageless

miracles," Erickson says. He leans over Niclaus and looks at me. "Most Technicians go in for all that stuff about leveling up when we die. It's this whole theory the bigwigs at the Academy started to make sure we'd never try to modify our elements by uploading ourselves. Me, I just know too much about what it's like to upload. You lose something, kid. They say you don't, but you do. Something maybe you don't notice, maybe no one can see. You're you—all of your brain's quantum states—but there's something missing." He shivers. "I don't believe I'm gonna live forever in some higher plane, but I sure don't want to live forever in a lower one."

"Amen," Niclaus says.

"And thank spitballs."

Niclaus waves a hand at Erickson and shakes his head. This looks like an exchange these men have had a million times. They've probably spent years traveling the universe together, debating religion and the nature of the universe, and . . . and being free. Being able to step out of their homes and onto this spaceship and have no daddies. Who cares what the universe is like? It only matters if you can explore it. Otherwise the universe is nothing but a room in a house and a locked door. And yet I do care. I want to know. I want to find a way to see everything I had to leave.

Erickson releases his straps, pushes a button on

his chair, and swivels to face us. "Now we have an hour before we get to Earth using old-fashioned nuclear propulsion. So, the question for you two is, how are you going to hide the kid? Because if you don't have a plan that holds water, you'll be walking off the ship and into a security transport straight back to the Academy. I'll carry you in a gear bag if I have to, and if you think you can get away from me, think again."

"Maybe that's the solution," Niclaus says.

"Stand up." Erickson waves at me, and I climb out of the chair. He's right: there's no way I could get away from him, or anybody else. Maybe he'd be bigger and stronger than me if I was a grown woman, but at least then I'd have a fighting chance. I look up at him and wait while he gives a me a once-over. "Security is looking for weapons, not people. Nobody's trafficking girls *to* Earth."

"We just need to get her far enough away from the ship that no one knows she came off it," Niclaus says.

"She'll fit in the case for the hazmat suits."

"What happens when the scan shows I'm not suits?" I ask. I've read about security scans, thanks to Camilla.

They both look at me.

"She's right," Erickson says. "It'll never work." He folds his arms and stares down at me.

My heart pounds. I'm so close. Earth is out there.

I never even had time to imagine what being free could mean.

"I'm going to walk out with her," Niclaus says. "We're just going to walk out." He folds his arms too, and the two men look over me at each other. I have the urge to run for it, to just go, to just try to find an exit or a hiding place. But I know Niclaus is my best chance. And he's about to give up something for me. I don't exactly understand how. I don't know what will happen if he walks a strange little girl out of here. "She could have gotten into the port somehow. Stranger things have happened. Those security guys don't have enough information to guess the truth."

As we're talking, the big blue ball that must be Earth is coming closer. A whole universe that might be closed to me.

I don't want Niclaus to sacrifice something huge for me. What Daddy did to me is not his fault. I can see in his face now that if he walks me out, somebody will make him pay. Maybe this is the time for me to be selfish, but not with Niclaus, not with the person who saved me. There has to be another solution.

"Can you take me to another colony?" I ask. "Any-where." I try to keep the pleading out of my voice. I hate that my voice is a little kid's. But Niclaus's face twists. He looks like he might cry, and I try to remember if I've ever seen a man look that way, but I don't think I have. Daddy cried when Vera didn't work, but his face never looked like this. Daddy's face was red when he cried. Niclaus's face is gray.

"It's not my ship," Niclaus says. "We can only go where Clawhammer sends us."

"What if I stay here on the ship until they send you somewhere? I don't need food. I mean, I need it or I'll feel like I'm starving, but I don't *need* it. If you're right about my parameters being the same as before, I'll live through anything. It doesn't matter how long." As I say this, hope surges through me. I'll live. I will. No matter what happens, no matter whether somebody catches me. In this universe, I have superpowers. I'm invincible.

"There's some food," Erickson says. "But we've got several jobs to do on Earth. It's possible they'll reassign the ship."

"Not likely," Niclaus says. "We have an off-world assignment in less than in a month."

Minutes pass as the three of us stare at each other, contemplating our options. I know this is my best chance, a way for me to eventually blend into this universe without hurting Niclaus. The men realize it too.

"Okay," Erickson says. "Nice to meet you, kid. I hope you have a nice life." He walks away from the console, through the open center of the control room, and out a door. He closes it behind him, and we hear a decisive click, as if he's locking us in here with finality. But I know Niclaus won't be here for long. Soon, I'll be alone on this ship.

"I'll show you where the food and water is," Niclaus says. Tears well at the edges of his eyes. "It's not a lot. We don't spend more than a couple days on assignment, and usually we're on a planet with a colony."

"It's enough," I say.

"It isn't."

"Yes, it is." I know it will hurt. If they're gone for a long time, it might be the worst pain I've ever experienced. Maybe I can't even imagine how hard it will be. But I'll survive it, and I won't be with Daddy.

"It's possible Clawhammer might change my assignment. If that happens, I won't be able to come back."

"It's fine, Niclaus. Thank you."

Niclaus slowly kneels down, one knee after the other. It's something adults do to talk to children, but I can see that he's doing it not because I'm a child, but because he wants to talk to me as an equal. I see in his eyes that he doesn't want to leave me.

"I'm so sorry this happened to you," Niclaus says. "The company never should have done the contract that way. Usually these universes are communal. The company creates them and sells spots. They aren't built for one group. Even Pocket Parts doesn't give an individual control over another human element.

Everyone would have to agree. It just doesn't happen." His speech gets faster at the end, and then he pauses for a few seconds. "I think about my daughter. About how a father could do that."

"I can tell you're a good father," I say. "Go home and give her a hug."

Tentatively, Niclaus reaches out and pulls me in to a hug. I wrap my arms around his neck. I can't remember the last time I hugged another person and meant it. Yes, I can. It was Samantha, on the last day. I close my eyes and rest my head on Niclaus's shoulder, and I tell myself that I will not die, that I have time to figure out a way to save her. I have time to figure out how to save myself, how to upload myself and change my parameters so I can grow. Now that I know it's all possible, nobody can prevent me from doing it.

I'm going to live here, and I'm going to learn, and I'm going to find a way to rescue Samantha and everyone else from Daddy. I have all the time in the universe.

14

THE PAIN SHOOTS THROUGH ME, and I can't see anything. I thought it would be short, that I'd scream
and hurt, and then it would be over. Then there
would be no more pain. But it keeps going and going,
and I press my hands into the floor, and I feel that
my hands are there. I curl the rug in my fingers, and
I know it's Daddy's rug. I'm still here, still in pain,
and I don't understand why it didn't work, or hasn't
worked yet. Could Daddy have done something to
make the pain last longer, knowing I'd do this?

I want it to stop. To just stop.

After some time, after minutes, maybe, it does. I
slump to the floor, and now I realize I'm keeping my
eyes closed. I could open them, but I don't want to. I
don't want to see the rug beneath me or the interface
floating in the air or the door. Most of all I don't want
to see Daddy, because he must be there. He must be

standing still and silent, watching me hurt, glad for it.

Tears leak out from behind my eyes. I'm not going to move any more, not ever. He can pick me up if he wants to. He can carry me around all day like a limp sack of tubers. I won't do anything anymore.

"Ella," a soft voice whispers. It's a woman's voice, one I don't recognize.

I don't move. I press my fingers into the rug. I squeeze my eyes shut.

"Ella, I'm so sorry. I know it hasn't been any time for you, and you thought you wanted to die, but I don't believe you did. I couldn't let you." The voice is kind, but I don't trust that. She's saying she knew I wanted to die. The implications dawn on me. Deleting myself worked, or would have worked, but somebody stopped me. This woman stopped me.

I push myself up, ready to scream, ready to leap on this woman. But the look in her eyes holds me back. She's kneeling next to me, and I don't know her, but there's something familiar about her long face, her dark hair and thick eyebrows. Her eyes are wet as if she's holding back tears, and she looks truly happy to see me.

"Who are you?" I ask instead. Tears leap from my eyes and roll down my cheeks. Behind her is the door to the office, which is open a few inches. Any second, Daddy could come through that door.

"He's not coming," the woman says. "It's okay."

I stare at her, waiting for an answer to the question I asked.

"I'm Kady," the woman says. She brushes a piece of hair away from her face. I notice long fingernails carefully rounded, a bracelet on the wrist, a mole on the left cheek. My brain rushes through a chain of thoughts. This woman looks like she's in her thirties. If this is Kady, then time has passed. Twenty years or a hundred or a thousand. If this is Kady, then deleting myself *worked*. Then Daddy suffered. Then I was free. I got away from him.

And now I'm back.

I wipe the tears from my eyes. I *was* free. That's something.

"There's a lot you need to know," Kady says. "The first thing is, I wasn't supposed to bring you back yet. I was supposed to wait until the entire team was here. Everyone we've brought back, it's been a process. We all agreed. But I couldn't let you face everyone and hear what happened with all of those. . . ." She shakes her head. "With people in your face, wanting something."

"Samantha," I say.

"Not yet," Kady says. Her eyes flit away from me.

"But you can." I lift myself to my feet, and Kady stands as well. She brushes dust off her knees. I look up at her. "You figured out how to save the people Daddy deleted."

"Yes, we did. But Ella, a lot has happened."

"Tell me." I fold my arms over my chest. I'm too aware that I'm still wearing pajamas. Now even Kady is bigger than me. But I'm not going to act like I'm five, not with Kady, and not with anyone. I'm done with all of that, no matter what's about to come out of her mouth.

Kady takes a deep breath. She runs a hand through her hair. "So, after you deleted yourself, Phil pretty much lost his mind. He locked himself in here trying to figure out how to get you back. But he couldn't. He just didn't know enough about the system. So he was in here for months and months. People were trying to get pregnant. And what we didn't know until then was that Phil had to actively approve births. Like, when a woman gets pregnant, he got a notification or something, and then he would approve it so the baby could grow."

She shakes her head. "It's disgusting. Nobody agreed to that. But while he was in here, he wasn't approving any births. So people started coming here, demanding that he approve their pregnancies. But he wouldn't. He wouldn't do anything but try to find you. And try to make Vera. He made so many Veras." Kady shudders, and so do I. She pauses for a few long seconds. "People got angry. They came here in a group, right in this room, and they got mad, and—my mom was here—and he deleted all of them."

"Briana," I say. It was just yesterday that I saw her, and she tried to help me. She gave me those manuals.

"Yes. He deleted my mom. And so my dad led another group here, and they got him away from the interface, and they locked him up in the meeting house. All the adults agreed not to let him out until he agreed to approve births, and there was a huge debate about how to punish him for deleting people, and for hiding this stuff he put in the contract. But they couldn't agree, and he was just there locked up, and nobody could have children, and that's what it was like while I was growing up."

"How long has it been?" I ask. I've been trying to gauge the answer from her eyes, from her demeanor, from her voice, but I can't tell. I'm guessing it's been maybe thirty years because she seems young to me— so much younger than her mother did.

"Fifty years," Kady says.

"I was free for fifty years." I try to appreciate what that means.

"My mom was dead for fifty years." Kady's jaw hardens. Her eyes fill with tears again.

"I didn't do this to hurt anyone," I say. "But she could have helped more. Everyone could have helped more. They could have locked him up because he was hurting *me*. They could have done something all those years."

"A person here, a person there. Most people didn't

lose their babies or their mothers," Kady says. "He told those stories about people moving to the Western Settlement. I guess it was easier to pretend to believe." Her bitterness meets mine, and I remember that she was a child when Daddy was hurting me. "But they did do something, finally. Thanks to my dad. And then they made a deal with Phil because they still wanted their people back, but they needed Phil to let them into the system. So they agreed that if Phil would let them in, they would try to bring you back as well as everyone else."

My whole body runs cold. I'm the sacrifice. Again. I turn toward the interface. It's open. I can find myself. I can delete myself again.

"No!" Kady grabs me by both shoulders. "Ella, I won't let Phil have you. That's why I'm here."

"No!" I struggle in her grip. I kick with my little feet, which does nothing.

Kady reaches up with one hand and touches something, and Daddy's interface goes dark. "You need the code to get back in, Ella," Kady says. "You can't delete yourself again. I'm trying to help you. You didn't want to die. I don't believe that. Remember when we used to play together? The day the Technician came, we played on the swings. Do you remember that?"

"Of course I remember," I snap. My face is burning. I have to think of something to do that will hurt her, or that will hurt myself. Something that will make sure they can't trade me to Daddy. "What are they going to do, lock me in the meeting house with Daddy? Let him come back to this house now that you have who you want? Do you have your mom back?"

"Yes, we saved her." Kady says. "We worked, all of us. My dad and his generation and later my generation too. We used the manuals in the database. We taught ourselves the basics. We figured it out. We brought every adult back. We did it."

But not Samantha. I see in her eyes, in the way they flit away from me again, that there's a reason for that. They want me to do something.

"But we still can't have any births," Kady says. "Not without Phil."

"No."

Kady's head falls. She lets go of me. "I know it's a lot to ask you to even see him. We talked about not bringing you back yet, about waiting ten more years for the Technician to come and asking him to help us. But someone did ask Niclaus to help. Camilla asked him to bring her family back, and he said he couldn't do it because it would violate the contract."

"She asked him?"

"Yes, and so we can't count on help from outside. We have to help ourselves. We agreed. . . ."

"To give me to Daddy so you can have babies again."

"Not give you to him, just let him see you."

"That will never be enough for him. He won't do what you want unless I act like Ella."

"I don't know," Kady says.

"And no one will save Samantha until Daddy gives you your births, right? Because you need to have something over me."

Kady sighs and looks away. "None of this was my decision. I just wanted to save you." She meets my eyes again. "Someday you'll want to be alive. I know you will. Someday we'll figure out how to beat Phil completely."

I walk past her. I walk out of the office and into the hallway. It's like I remember it. There's no indication that time has passed. I walk through the living room, and Daddy's furniture is still there. There's a sofa that looks as new as it did fifty years ago.

Kady is behind me. "The plan was to bring you back tomorrow," Kady says. "You don't have to let anyone know you're back yet."

"I don't have to do anything," I say.

"No, of course not. You can stay with me. Or get your own house. Whatever you want."

I know she knows I can't do that. Daddy won't help them have their babies if I go live in some house somewhere and have my own life. If they managed to lock up Daddy, they can lock me up too. I don't know if it's nice of her to pretend or if it's cruel. I want to believe that she truly thinks I'll want to live.

But one more day won't help anything.

"I'm going to see Daddy." I don't look behind me to see her reaction. I just walk out the door and down the front steps. It's morning, and the air is misty. The birds are singing. The sun is large and bright, and even though to me no time has passed, I still missed the air and the sky of Bella Inizio. I breathe easier now that I'm out of the house, and I know that no matter what happens, I'm not going back in there. Never will I ever set foot in Daddy's house again, no matter what he does to me. The whole colony can turn against me, and I'll bash in my own head before I let them drag me back here.

Kady pulls up alongside me. "Are you sure you—"

"Yes." I keep walking. I feel taller. I was dead, and it didn't hurt for very long. I was free. Daddy couldn't touch me for fifty years. I need to see that he knows that. I need to see that he knows I won. I need to see him realize that he'll never beat me again, because I'll find a way to stop him. I was too small and weak to hurt him, but he can't have what he wants from me without my help. I won't be five-year-old Ella.

The first person to recognize me is a woman who's outside working in her garden. She lifts her head and calls out my name. I don't answer, and she runs inside. She must be getting on the walkie-talkie to tell everyone that I'm back, and sure enough, soon people flow out of their houses. Men and women come running out. Some are dressed, some are wearing nightclothes, some are wearing robes or boxers or slips.

Ella!

Kady!

Kady, what did you do?

Ella, what happened to you? Ella, why did you do it? Ella, Ella!

Kady puts her arm around me. "It's okay," she says. "I won't let them touch you."

All the people appear to be the same age. There are no children with them. A surge of emotion runs through me. It feels wrong, and yet I'm happy about it. They had children for sixty years because I stayed a child. They could have locked up Daddy before I left, but they didn't. They didn't help me, and I wasn't here to help them, and I love it. I smile, and then I laugh, and then I begin to run. I open my arms wide, and I run down the middle of the street. I turn a corner, and the meeting house is in front of me, and there are people behind me and more coming out of their houses. It's like the day the Technician came, except there are no children, and I don't need help any more. They are the ones who need help. They need me, and they always needed me, but now I realize it. Now I understand that without me they have nothing.

15

I REACH THE MEETING HOUSE, and I turn around and face the crowd. I'm a little girl in my pajamas, but I'm not. They know I'm not.

"I'm Ella Harkin, and I'm back!" I yell. "I came to see Phil Harkin because I want to see him locked away. I'm not going to do anything he wants! I'm not going to do anything you want!"

All the people blend together with their ageless faces, until Camilla steps out of the crowd. And she's not alone. A tall, dark-skinned man is with her.

"Darius!" I yell, pointing at him. "How do you like being alive?"

Darius puts his arm around Camilla, who is crying.

I walk toward them. "Are you crying because you didn't get everything you want?" I ask.

"I'm crying because you're alive," Camilla says. "I blamed myself." She reaches out for me, and for a second I let her hug me. I let her arms wrap around me, and I feel the warmth of someone who helped me. She did care. She gave me books to read. Without Camilla, I wouldn't really be grown up, I'd be a fifty-eight-year-old child with no education. If not for me, Daddy would never have deleted Darius, and they'd have their child.

"Did you agree to this plan?" I ask from inside her arms, from under her tears. "To hold back Samantha?"

Camilla doesn't say anything. I hear the answer in her tears. She did agree.

I pull away from her. "You didn't know Samantha," I say, "because you were just born when Daddy killed her. You didn't know that she was kind and generous and patient. You didn't know that she could love anyone, even Daddy. She saw the good in people. And she stood up to him. She was the only person in my whole life who stood up to Daddy for me. She told him to his face that he was doing the wrong thing, and that's why he killed her. You helped me in secret. You were too afraid. Until I was gone, you were all too afraid."

Behind me, the door to the meeting house rattles.

My heart races. I can't breathe. I turn toward the door, and Kady is beside me. Her hand is on my back.

"It's okay," she says. "Nobody will let him hurt you."

"Won't they?"

"I won't." Out of the corner of my eye, I see Briana and her husband, Nagesh. Briana has tears in her eyes, too, but they're happy tears. The two of them stand on the other side of me. "Well done, Kady," Briana says.

Nagesh moves forward and walks up the three wide steps to the front door. He turns back to me. "Do you want to see him?"

"Yes," I say. The answer is no. I don't want to see him. I want him to disappear and be gone forever without me ever having to encounter him. But if he's here, then I have to. He has to see that he can't hurt me. Until I show him, he'll never know.

What's the worst that can happen? I was already dead.

Nagesh puts a key in the lock and turns it. He walks back down the steps. We all stand on the street and look up at the door as the knob turns, as the door opens, as Daddy steps out.

He's wearing loose cloth pants and a shirt that's faded over years of wear. His hair is long over his ears. His eyes, as they seek me and find me, are aged. That's my first thought as our eyes meet over the several yards between us. His eyes are old. He's old. His youthful body can't hide it. He walks slowly down the steps toward me, and it's like the entire crowd is holding a breath. Kady's arm tightens around my shoulders. Briana tenses.

Daddy comes in front of me. He gets down on his knees and holds out his arms. He hasn't said a word yet. No one has said a word since Nagesh turned the key.

I remember when I was a little kid, when I was five, when Daddy was my whole world in a good way. I remember him reading books to me in bed, cooking me pancakes in funny shapes, taking me for walks outside in the woods. I remember the person who loved me. I look for that person in Daddy's old, old eyes. And I see him. I know that somewhere, there's a man who once lost a child.

My stomach churns, and I want to vomit.

Daddy suddenly lunges forward to grab me.

Kady and Briana both step in front of me, but Daddy is faster. Daddy has me in his arms. Bile rises in my throat. I put a hand over my mouth. Daddy's chest presses against the hand, against my face. The world is closing in on me, and people are talking or screaming or crying or all of that, but all I feel is the need to throw up, and my stomach convulses, and I push away from him. I push him so hard that I fall back, and I turn away just in time to vomit in front of Briana's feet.

"Ella," Daddy says. His hands are on his knees now. His hair is falling in his face. "Why did you do that? Why did you leave me?"

"Because you hurt me," I say.

"I never—"

"Because you hurt all these people. You deleted people. You deleted babies. You're a monster."

Daddy reaches out a hand. "Let's go home, Ella. Let's make everything the way it was."

"Please, Ella," someone says from behind me. It's a man's voice, pleading. The pain of all the lost years is in that voice. The pain of all the children who aren't here. All I have to do to help this man is go back to the way things used to be. All I have to do is forget that there was ever a way to escape, that there were ever fifty years where I won.

"Never," I whisper. I say it only loud enough for Daddy to hear. I look up into Daddy's eyes. "Never never never never." I take a deep breath, and then I take a step back.

Daddy's eyes harden. His jaw clenches. All the muscles in his body tighten, and I know he's about to spring. He's about to leap toward me and grab me. Briana and Kady and Nagesh all tense, as if they're about to jump on him. And then:

Daddy disappears.

There's no noise, no warning, and nothing left. Daddy is gone.

A woman is standing about a foot back from where Daddy was. She's about five foot six and thin, and her hair is cropped short. She's wearing a green jumpsuit with a patch on one front pocket with a large, stylized T. She looks to be about the same age as all of the colonists appear to be.

Her eyes find mine, and she smiles big. "I wish I could say I was surprised," she says, as if we're the only two people on the street. "But when I saw your code in there, I knew exactly what these people had done. Tell me I'm wrong. Tell me they didn't just try to sell you to Daddy to save their asses."

I examine her eyes, her hair color, her cheekbones, her mouth. My heart is beating so fast I can barely think. I see her. I know her. But how can this be?

"When I tried to delete myself, Niclaus saved me," the other version of myself says. She looks over my head and raises her voice. "I guess I can tell you folks, since you're never getting out of here. The real world is a simulation too! Niclaus took me out, I trained to be a Technician, leveled myself down to modify my parameters, back up again. None of this means shit to you guys. I came back here at great expense to myself to help anyone who deserved helping, and what do I find? You guys have pulled a version of me from backup just to torture her some more. Is that right, Ella?"

"Yes." I can't stop looking at her face. *My* face. She's what I've always wanted to be. She is me. She got out. I take a step forward. I hang on the words she says next.

"Well, I guess that's it then. You want to come with me, Ella? I can modify you to grow up, look exactly like me. Is that what you want?"

"Yes," I say. And then: "Can I have long hair?"

Ella laughs. "Sure. You can look like anyone you want."

"I want to look like me," I say. "Like you. I just want to grow up." I walk toward her. I want to hug her, but it seems so weird that I don't. I just stop in front of her, and then I turn to face the crowd.

Camilla steps forward. "Did you really get out, Ella?" she asks. "Is this real?"

Ella smiles at Camilla, and there's malice in it. I can almost hear her thoughts, and I feel like she can hear mine. Just a little more courage. Just a little more effort. Just a little less willingness to sacrifice me for all of them. It would have been so easy for the entire colony to band together to help me, but they wanted what Daddy could give them.

"What do you think, Ella?" Ella asks, making sure her voice is loud enough to be heard. "Should we give them back their children, or no?" She laughs for a moment. "I can make the wind destroy you! I can turn the trees into water! I can reverse gravity. I'm already breaking the contract by deleting Daddy. Not to mention the Technician's Creed. *We will never harm a human under our care.* Remember that, Ella?"

For a moment, my hate surges. I want Ella to do those things. I want to see these people washed away. I want them to suffer. But I know Ella is only joking. I know that because she's me. She doesn't want to hurt anybody. She just wants everyone to know she can.

"I want them to have their children," I say. I don't say it loudly. I don't care if they hear me, and maybe I want them not to. Maybe I want them to wonder for a little bit longer, to worry that they'll have to live in a universe that isn't the paradise they wanted. Maybe I want them to hurt just a little bit more.

"Ella, oh Ella." Briana hugs the other me, and the other me hugs her back. There are tears in both women's eyes.

"Do you want to come with us?" Ella asks.

"Oh, thank you, but no," Briana says. "I love Bella Inizio. I have my garden and my husband and my daughter. With Phil gone, we have a chance to have such a beautiful world."

"What about you, Kady?" Ella asks. "Want to see the next level up?"

"Yes," Kady says, "but no. My mom's right. Without Phil, this is our universe."

Now it's Camilla's turn to hug Ella. I'm a little bit surprised that Ella is so willing to hug her back, but maybe time has changed her. Maybe time has made her appreciate what Camilla did for us before she stopped helping. Maybe someday I'll be able to appreciate that too.

"I'm so sorry, Ella," Camilla says.

"I'm sorry that Daddy hurt you because of me," Ella replies. "But I don't know if I can forgive all of you for letting me suffer. The only reason I won't hurt anyone, the reason I'm going to put the universe right, is because there are good humans. Samantha existed. Niclaus existed. Because of them, I'm here today. I'm going to give this universe a chance to make more good people." She's smiling as she says it, but her eyes are hard. I know she's doing the right thing, but it isn't easy. I don't want them to be happy, but the other me is right. There are good people waiting to be born here. And maybe good people who can still be made from these cowards.

Ella looks down at me. "Is there anything else you want to do?"

I shake my head. "I want to find out what's out there."

"Okay, give me just a minute or two." Ella waves at the crowd. Then she stands still and looks across the city, taking in Bella Inizio for one last time. Her eyes well up, and one hand goes over her mouth, and I know what she's thinking. It's beautiful—it really is. It's an amazing, precious, perfect planet that we could have been lucky to call home.

She disappears, and for a long minute, I wonder

if I dreamed her. Could it be that I'm still dead, or that I'm dying, and the idea that I might escape is all fiction?

Kady wraps her arms around me, and I grab on to her shoulders.

"Come back and say hello someday," she says.

And then I'm standing in a dark room, and there's the sound of humming, and there are machines all around me, and I look down at myself, and I'm looking down from higher off the ground. I look straight into the eyes of my doppelganger, and tears are rolling down her face.

She grabs me and pulls me close, and I can barely breathe. We're both weeping, just bawling our eyes out like little children in this strange room.

"Samantha," I choke out. "She's still in there."

"Yes, she is." The other me pulls back and wipes her face on her sleeve. "Stand back a little bit." She waves me toward a path through the large, humming boxes: the servers that contain Bella Inizio and everyone I've ever known. I run my hand through my long hair and look down at the tall body that I have now. I'm wearing the same pajamas I was wearing before, except bigger, and I open my palms wide and stare at my large hands. I gawk at my slippered feet, my woman's curves, my existence. I don't know whether to scream or leap into the air with joy. I'm so happy and so terrified.

The other me is standing in the middle of an interface. There are numbers floating around her, and she has things stuck to her head, and she waves her arms. It's so much more than I ever learned by watching Daddy, and I realize that Daddy didn't know anything. Daddy couldn't do anything. Daddy was just a man who wanted to live like a twentieth-century person on a planet he owned. Daddy might not even have been very smart.

It's taking a long time, and I don't want to wait, but then I realize that Ella must be giving the colonists back their children, putting the universe right again, eliminating Daddy's special permissions. She's keeping her promise to the colonists, even though she doesn't have to. She wipes sweat from her face.

"So that part's done. Camilla is pregnant."

We lock eyes, and hers are bitter. But we both know it's the right decision. We both want Bella Inizio to be a place where people can be happy. It's our home, and these are people we've known our whole lives. They're not bad people, just bad for us.

Ella turns back to the interface, and this time, it doesn't take long.

Out of nowhere, Samantha appears.

She's on the ground, screaming. Her reddish brown hair falls over her face, and she takes a deep breath, and the other me is on the ground with her, and the two of them are rocking together.

I fall to my knees and crawl toward them, and Samantha is touching the other me's face and saying our name, and she sees me, and for a moment there's confusion, but then she laughs, and then we're all laughing. We're all on our knees on the ground laughing our heads off as tears roll down our faces.

16

As the three of us walk out into the real Bella Inizio sun, I can't help but think about the day almost fifty years ago when I walked out of this building for the first time with Niclaus. Then, there was no time to consider the life I was stepping into. All I wanted was out, and I would have done anything to get away. I didn't have time to worry about getting revenge on Daddy. But now, I've deleted him and all his backups. I've erased Phil Harkin more completely than if I'd dug him up and burned his bones.

There was a part of me that wanted to see him again before I did it. I wanted to look into his eyes and make sure he saw that it was me who was doing it. But you can't delete somebody so thoroughly from inside. I had to be out here to be sure that every scrap of him would be gone. I have to be content with the fact that I found his code and swiped it away, and then I dug for backups, and I checked again and again and again to be sure that none of him was left. I have to trust everything that I learned from the Academy and believe that I have the skills to wipe an element from existence.

I just wish the memories of what he did to me could be deleted so easily.

Now that fifty more years have passed on the planet, some of the foliage has come back. Clawhammer got what they wanted from this part of the planet, and their operations are on the southern hemisphere now. So maybe it will be possible for people to live on Bella Inizio again someday. The ruins of the original Harkin Town are more ruined. Buildings have fallen farther in on themselves. But now there really are trees growing amid the rubble.

"Phil was a good person once," Samantha says.

"Other people's families died," Ella says. "No one else did what he did."

"I never thought there was a good time to tell you, because you were still a kid, but Vera and Ella weren't the first family Phil lost." Samantha stares in the direction of the ruins of Harkin Town as she talks. "Back on Earth, right before the discovery of space-folding technology, things were bad. There were about twenty years when people were just dropping dead. The environment was ruined. You couldn't breathe without risking something." She looks up at the sky, and as she pauses, I breathe in the Bella Inizio air. It's better than it was when I first leveled up, but it hasn't completely recovered. It will never be as good as the environment inside the simulation.

"Phil had another wife and two children. The children were teenagers when they died. And I had lost my parents and my brother. Almost everyone who came to Bella Inizio had lost someone."

I remember that Samantha's son, Davin, is in the graveyard, one of the unlucky ones who never had a chance to upload into a place that was safe, and I put my arm around her. I'm taller than she is now, and I press my head against hers.

"Maybe the sudden appearance of faster-than-light travel was our creators' way of rescuing us," Samantha says.

I shake my head. "Please don't say that."

"Why not? You've just explained that the real world is also a simulation."

"The Technician who rescued me, Niclaus, believed in a creator a level up. He believed so strongly that this creator was going to level him up when he died that he refused to upload himself. Technicians at the top level secretly do it to extend their lives. They upload and then level themselves back up again. That's how I was able to change my parameters and become an adult. It's highly unauthorized, but it would have saved his life, and he wouldn't do it. He wouldn't even upload himself into any of a million simulations where he could have gone for free. He just chose to die." I vow that I'm not going to cry for Niclaus in front of Samantha and my other self. I don't want to burden them with the last fifty years of my life. Not yet.

I just wish Niclaus could be here to see me finally succeed. I wish he could have lived to see his daughter, Talia, become Vice Chancellor of the Academy. I wish he wouldn't have wasted himself on an unprovable theory.

There's so much to see in this universe. This universe is practically infinite. And contrary to fears among the Academy elite, those of us formerly trapped elements who have escaped haven't ruined the universe yet. It turns out that a lot of people just want to get out of universes that have become prisons. They don't want to take their war games and chocolate rivers with them. They want to live like ordinary humans in the universe we've always known—the one people are born in, live in, and die in without ever leaving.

When I killed Daddy and made all those changes to Bella Inizio, I made myself a fugitive. I broke the Technician's Code, and worse, I breached the Academy's contract with Clawhammer. If the Chancellor catches me, she'll have me uploaded somewhere horrific. That's what they do to criminals now, and there's a special hell for rogue Technicians.

So I have nothing left to lose. From now on, I'm going to dedicate my long, healthy life to helping other people like me. I'm not going to wait to be assigned to perform duties on a contract with Clawhammer or Pocket Parts—as dictated by them and the universe owners. I'm going to seek out universes wherever they are, enter them, and ask if anybody needs help. I'm going to save anyone who wants to be saved, whether they can pay for it or not.

Nobody is going to be in the situation I was in because some man signed an agreement with a huge corporation. The Chancellor and all the Academy bigwigs who want to keep their funding and their special privileges can go fuck themselves. They may have become their own law over the years—but this universe is big. Let them try to come and get me.

First, I show Samantha and the other me the graveyard. Ella and I leave Samantha at Davin's grave for a moment and walk to visit our own family. We stand looking down at the grave of a little girl named Ella who never got to have a life.

"She was probably nothing like us," Ella says.

"We do have the same genetic parents."

"She had Daddy before he was crazy."

I wonder if that's true—if Daddy was already crazy because of the other family he lost, or if he was never crazy but was just evil. Or if he wasn't evil but was a normal variation of human. I wonder if I should have known for sure exactly what was wrong with him before I killed him.

"You did the right thing," the other me says, reading my mind.

"Thank you for saying that." We stare at each other, taking in the weirdness.

She reaches for me and pulls me into a hug. "Thank you for coming back for me."

"I didn't know you were there," I say. But I hold on to her. We hold each other close as if we're long-lost sisters, as if we knew that we'd lost each other, as if we've been waiting for this moment for a hundred years.

Samantha approaches us, tears in her eyes. "I never thought I'd see this place again, and I was okay with that. But I'm so glad I got to visit him."

Ella and I each take one of Samantha's hands, and we take a walk through Harkin Town. It feels necessary to see what the original colony has become. I think I need to see this to leave again, to understand that there truly is nothing left on my home for me. We walk through what's left of Daddy's house and we visit the remains of the meeting hall, where the colonists finally locked up Daddy. There's nothing left of him here. They're just ruins.

"Want to see the world's smallest spaceship?" I ask. "It's a lot like the one Daddy came on when he claimed the homestead." This is the kind of ship Clawhammer sends when someone suffers a medical emergency—like if Niclaus had caught the gastro from his trip to Bella Inizio. The kind they have rows and rows of on several different planets.

We cycle through the airlock, even though with the three of us being immune from disease, it's unnecessary, and then we enter the cramped crew quarters/ bridge. It's just one small room. Everything else is in support of the ship's AI, which either actually folds space in violation of the expected laws of physics or pretends to. Either way, it will take us where we want to go.

"I stole the ship," I tell them. "So I won't be going back to working for the Academy."

"You were a real Technician?" Ella asks.

"Yep. I learned everything. Certified for all levels, from making a bird sing to creating a universe."

Ella's smile is sad. "You gave all that up?"

"It was worth it," I say.

I explain my situation to Samantha and Ella, leaving out most of the details of my life. I tell them that I went to the Academy but gloss over how I got there and exactly when I became adult-sized. I skip over most of my life with Niclaus, except to say that he became like a father to me. But I don't make it through that simple line without letting tears escape.

"There's a lot more you haven't told us," Samantha says, putting her arm around me.

"Yes, but for now. . . ." I pull myself together. "I want you to know what I'm planning. Because I can take you anywhere you want to go. Back to Earth, to another colony. I can even find you another simulation if that's what you want." I tell them about my plan to help other trapped elements.

"If we get caught by the Chancellor, she could pretty much do anything to us," I caution. "She could stuff us in any simulation. Starve us for a thousand years. Her power is limitless. She doesn't want us to do this because she doesn't want people outside her control to know the truth. Knowledge is transmissible. It's dangerous to her. It's dangerous to us too—Niclaus wasn't lying about the possible problems. It's just that they haven't happened yet. Maybe they will. Maybe if I save other people, we'll end up living in a universe that's pure chaos. But I have to do this. I can't let anyone else suffer the way we did."

Ella, who has been pacing around the tiny space, stops and examines herself in the shininess of the bulkhead. "We can't let anyone else suffer," she says. She turns to face us and stuffs her hands into the pockets of her ridiculous pajamas. "I'm never going to be afraid of anyone again. Nobody like Daddy will ever have any power over me. Nobody like Daddy can ever have power over anyone. It sounds like this Chancellor person is like Daddy."

"Yes and no," I say. "I'm afraid of her, but she won't stop me."

"Then I'm in," Samantha says. "I think doing something brave with my new life sounds like just the ticket."

"You were always brave," Ella says.

We all three are silent, thinking about what Samantha did for us. She spoke the truth to someone who wanted lies. If everyone in our universe did that, then the people doing it wouldn't be deleted. The people doing it would win.

And if everyone helped someone that rules and regulations required them not to help, a whole lot more people would be happy.

I pick up the old spaceman helmet that had fallen onto the deck and put it back in its rightful place, in the seat next to me. I may not be able to have Niclaus, but I can remember him. Since he let himself die, it's the best I can do.

"Strap in," I say to Ella and Samantha, pointing to the row of seats that line the small circular room. "Be aware—you might want to upchuck." I tell the AI to launch, and I turn on the viewscreen so we can look down at the planet like I did with Niclaus and Erickson all those years ago.

"It's beautiful," Samantha says.

Ella looks away. She folds her arms over her chest, and her hair falls into her face. I guess waking up to find she wasn't dead after all changed the way she looks at our planet. I try to imagine how I would have felt if I had woken up back in Daddy's office instead of here in this universe, and I don't want to.

Samantha puts her arm around Ella. "But we never have to come back here."

"It's not that," Ella says. "I always wanted to get out, but only because of Daddy. I don't know if I want to leave everything. But I can't stand to be here now."

"Then let's find another place to go," I say. I instruct the AI to jump us to the farthest inhabited planet yet discovered. They have a growing civilization and plenty of pocket universes. It's the perfect place to dip our toes into checking on our fellow trapped elements.

Bella Inizio disappears, and we reappear somewhere else.

AFTERWORD

Thank you so much for reading my simulated-universe book!

This story has many sources of inspiration and has been through many iterations. I first learned about the theory that if we ever manage to create a simulated universe, we are probably in one, at a Northeast Conference on Science and Skepticism circa 2012. The idea is that if we can create an essentially infinite number of universes within our own, there are likely to be infinitely more simulated universes than there are real ones (even though there may be infinite real ones)—therefore the odds are in favor of any given universe, including our own, being a simulation. Of course in reality this idea is completely untestable, so it's just fun to think about.

In this story I posit that if we were suddenly able to violate the laws of physics in an extreme way, like if we discovered a super-convenient faster-than-light drive, that might be proof that our reality is simulated. In Ella's world, if they didn't already know they were in a simulation, they would have discovered the truth when they realized that not all the heavenly bodies they can see from Bella Inizio are actually reachable at the same time. Some have speculated that Heisenberg's uncertainty principle is evidence that we're in a simulation—there just isn't enough storage space for us to know everything all at once.

In this story, the technicians prove that our world is a simulation when they're able to move elements from simulations they created into our universe, thus creating something out of nothing—another violation of a fundamental law. If we're all just elements in a program, then we would be able to move them as long as the systems were compatible. And if our universe is modeled on some other, "real" universe, with similar laws and similar beings, we might just invent the same type of system we're already in. Lucky for Ella, that's the case in *One Level Down*.

Too bad for everyone else that with too much movement of elements, we could end up with a bunch of non-sequitur chaos-producing nonsense along with our faster-than-light travel. I'd love to be able to explore what might happen if the technicians' fears come true, as well as what happens to the Ellas in the future, more of what happened to

Ella 1.0 after she escaped, and what (if anything) happened to Niclaus when he died. Maybe I'll get a chance to do that sometime in the future.

This story itself came about through the usual process of idea revision and expansion that takes something maybe a little bit interesting and turns it into something that hopefully works.

I originally envisioned a planet with the ruins of a colony, where all of the colonists, having found the real world too difficult, had retreated into a simulation. But I reasoned that someone would have to stay behind to take care of the equipment. At first, I thought the story lay with that person or group of people left behind. This evolved into the idea that corporations would exist that created universes and did the work of maintaining them. So I wrote a 10,000-word story about two technicians who came to a planet to do routine maintenance and were faced with the moral quandary of whether to help a person who was trapped inside. I just love a good moral quandary, and I gave Niclaus a juicy one. But as I was working on that story and even once it was done, Ella's character stayed in my brain.

As with most characters, I can't say for sure exactly why I created her. But I can say why I found her to be the most compelling person in the universe. I may not be trapped in the body of a little girl, but there was a time when I was. I viscerally remember people treating me like I was a silly little cute thing, and it's not like that treatment stopped when I grew up. I think being treated like you're stupid when you're the smartest person in the room is a pretty common experience for women and girls. Fortunately, if someone in real life is treating me like Daddy treats Ella, I can roll my eyes, catch an Uber to the home I own, and complain to my friends about it. Being forced to live under the thumb of that person would be my own personal horror story, so I empathize with everything Ella's going through. Putting characters through things you would hate to go through yourself is one of the true joys of writing. The worse the better for these poor characters!

The horrible irony for Ella is that she lives in a world where people can create anything they want—but she's stuck in a house with Daddy. She can't take advantage of any of it. What was just as interesting to me was the idea that Daddy and his cohort chose to live within a set of real-world constraints. They don't age or get sick, but they do have pain and suffering. They have normal human strength and have set limits on their technology.

If we really could create universes, I imagine that there would be lots of simulations that would be very weird, because of course people can be weird. Somebody would want to live in that war game or float along a chocolate river. But I don't think most people would choose weird. I think there's something fundamental about human nature that keeps us floating around in our fishbowls, oblivious to the ocean outside the glass.

If you are reading a science fiction book, you may be the kind of person who would choose something different, but I'm not so sure. I think it's harder to break free from the limits of our imagination than we might hope. I'm the one who wrote this book, and I have the same thing for breakfast every day. Most of the time I decide to come straight home from my day job and chill out rather than going somewhere and doing something. I text the same group chat every day. I listen to the same podcasts every week. You get the gist. I like to think I'm this interesting, creative person, but I'm stuck in my own fishbowl just like everyone else. What universe would I choose?

In the universe we actually live in, humans have almost limitless choices. As a species, we could live peacefully and sustainably. We probably can't eliminate work that sucks, but we could cut down on it a lot. We could provide housing for homeless people, food for the hungry, and health care for everyone. We could combine our resources to send a generation ship into space. We could cure aging and destroy all weapons. We don't have world peace because there are enough people in the world who don't want it— just like there are plenty of people who would choose to create a universe where they had power and control instead of a universe where everyone lived in total comfort. There are also plenty of people who would choose the universe with their favorite breakfast cereal over the universe where unicorns romp around pooping rainbows and people have superpowers.

There was a bit in my original story, which was from Niclaus's perspective, where he reminisced about a couple of men who created a universe just for themselves and their dog. That worked out for a few years, but then they stopped getting along and wanted out. Except they no longer had any living relatives who'd pay to have them moved, so Niclaus wasn't allowed to help them. It was kind of a joke about the horrors of other people (thank you, Sartre). But I imagined that there would be relatively cheap pocket universes all over the place in which people just didn't anticipate how to take care of all of their needs forever. I'm guessing that even your dog would make you crazy after a hundred years of togetherness.

All this is to say that whether they live in the real world or in a simulation, people who lack imagination end up suffering or making others suffer. Each of us, every day, can make an effort to turn our insignificant fishy heads toward the glass and take a look outside the bowl. Even if we're stuck in this one universe, there are infinite choices for how to live.

164

ACKNOWLEDGMENTS

Thank you to Jaymee Goh, Jacob Weisman, and the rest of the Tachyon team, including Jill Roberts, Kasey Lansdale, Rie Langdon, and Elizabeth Story, for their love and care in making this book a reality. To my agent, Jennifer Azantian, for her unwavering support for this project. To my critique group: Carolyn Ives Gilman, John Hemry, Simcha Kuritzky, Robert Chase, Michael LaViolette, Constance Warner and Bud Sparhawk; to Kelly Dwyer for introducing us; and to Aly Parsons for creating the group and welcoming me—I wish you were here to see this!

Thank you also to additional beta readers and friends Kristen Lippert-Martin, Madelyn Rosenberg, Wendy Fuller, and Brent Stricker, as well as the Washington, D.C., kidlit and sci-fi communities for their support and friendship. And thanks as always to my parents, Martha Greaney and John Thompson, for their unfailing support for my writing career. I would write even if I had no friends to share it with, but it's better to have them.

BOOK CLUB QUESTIONS

(Contains Spoilers)

1. In *One Level Down,* Ella knows she is in a simulated universe. Do you think Ella would have felt differently about her situation had she believed she was in the "real" world? If so, how?

2. Does Daddy have any redeeming qualities? Can you understand his motivation for his treatment of Ella?

3. The colonists of Bella Inizio have chosen to create a universe that is much like the real world. It includes pain, labor, and the basic inconveniences of life, but not aging past one's thirties or death. If you had to design a universe to live in, what would you design? Explain why.

4. Niclaus is in a difficult position because he knows he can rescue Ella from the simulation, but he isn't supposed to. Before Ella tries to delete herself, he is not planning to help her. Is this wrong? Why or why not?

5. It's revealed in the end that Niclaus allows himself to die in the "real" world instead of entering a simulation. What would you do?

6. After Ella tries to delete herself, her friend Kady pulls a copy of her from a backup. Who would you rather be: the original Ella or the backup version? If this happened to you, would you want to live and travel with the other version of you?

7. After escaping from the simulation, Ella pulls Samantha from a backup. Is this really Samantha, or is it her backup? Does it matter? Why or why not?

8. The Technicians know that the "real" world is a simulation, but they keep this knowledge secret. Is this wrong? Why or why not?

9. Should the colonists of Bella Inizio have done more to help Ella? Is their fear of Daddy's control over themselves and their families justification for not taking action against him? What would you do?

10. In the end, the colonists are left inside Bella Inizio without Daddy's control. Are they living in paradise or a nightmare? Were you surprised that Kady chooses to stay? Would you have chosen to leave with Ella if given the chance?

MARY G. THOMPSON is is the author of *The Word*, *Flicker and Mist*, and other novels for children and young adults. Thompson is originally from Eugene, Oregon, where she attended the University of Oregon School of Law. She is the author of *Wuftoom*, which Booklist called "absolutely unique." Her contemporary thriller *Amy Chelsea Stacie Dee* won the 2017 Westchester Fiction Award and was a finalist for the 2018–2019 Missouri Gateway Award. Her short fiction has appeared in *Dark Matter Magazine*, *Apex Magazine*, and others.

Thompson practiced law for seven years, including five years in the US Navy JAGC, and now works as a law librarian. She holds an MFA in Writing for

Children from The New School and completed the UCLA School of Theater, Film, and Television's Professional Program in Screenwriting.

Thompson lives in Washington, DC. Find her on the web at http://marygthompson.com.